For my lovely sister, Louise

SIMON AND SCHUSTER

First published in Great Britain in 2007 by Simon and Schuster UK Ltd,
A CBS COMPANY.

Simon & Schuster UK Ltd
Africa House, 64-78 Kingsway, London WC2B 6AH.

ISBN: 1-416-92670-4
EAN: 978-1-4169-2670-2

☆ Chapter One

I really don't want to be here. Stuck with these losers. Look at them! Useless! Queueing up in the dark, in the early morning outside this hotel. You can see they haven't got any talent. Not a drop. Not one of them.

They'll stand here waiting all day long. Until it's time to go inside and do more waiting. Hours and hours and hours inside the hotel lobby. Getting more and more nervous and excited.

We got here by taxi at five this morning. Five! It wasn't even light. That was Mam's fault. It's always Mam's fault. She's the one pushing us. She's the one with all the ambition, really. Eunice is ambitious, too, but she's lazy. If she had a choice, she wouldn't be catching taxis across town before dawn.

The taxi man thought we were mad. You could tell by his face. But he helped lug all of our stuff out of the house and into his cab. There was cases and

1

cases of it. All our showbiz gear. Everything we would need for the day. Eunice's costumes, and mine. And all the pots of paint and powder. The dark, sticky eyelashes and the smarmy lipsticks. And sequins like fish scales pulled off a mermaid. Mam always carries a box of spare sequins, so she can replace any that drop off our costumes. She sits sewing as we wait and wait and wait for our turn to audition.

Star Turn.

That's why we're here. That's why all these losers are here, too. Milling about outside this huge, posh hotel in the middle of our town. Millions of them! Well, hundreds maybe. Some of them are in costume already, like they can't wait to get going. They'll be all wrinkled by the time it's their turn. Others are in sleeping bags, lying on the pavement, holding their places near the front of the queue.

'What!' Mam shrieked, as the taxi slowed. 'I don't believe it! That's not fair! I booked this taxi as early as I could! I thought we'd be the first! I thought we'd be at the head of the queue! But look at them all! They must have been here all night!'

Mam was furious and amazed. She ushered us out of the taxi and we stood shivering by the kerb. The taxi's orange light was glaring in the bluey darkness as Mam went on and on, saying we should have been first in the queue. 'It's no good being at the back! Or somewhere in the middle! You need to be near the front! Before the judges get tired and cross! But it's too late! We've got here too late! I'm sorry, girls, but it's all been a waste of time! Already!'

Mam looked like she was about to go into one of her strops. A mega-strop. Right in front of the taxi driver and all the losers in the queue. We'd have to calm her down. I was too tired to think of anything. Our Eunice yawned hugely and said, 'No, Mam. I think it's good to be near the back of the queue. The judges will have seen loads of rubbish by the time we walk in, and they'll be so glad to see some genuine talent and star quality, we'll knock their socks off.'

I glanced up at my tall sister. What was she on about? Never mind, I thought. Her words were getting through to Mam, who was calming down and breathing more regularly.

Welcome to my family. This is typical us. Surrounded by our celebrity showbiz gear. Mam hyperventilating with panic. Eunice calming her down. Me scowling at them both. Not wanting to be there.

But I'm the one with the talent, you see.

*

So we ended up right near the end of the queue. Then other taxis started arriving thick and fast, depositing people of all ages. Kids and teenagers, mums and dads, grans and uncles and aunties and granddads. Mam bustled us into place, ready to jab anyone with her elbows if they looked like they were pushing in. Eunice lay down on our biggest case of showbiz gear and dozed off. Mam pleaded with her to wake up. To look her prettiest. To be ready to sing, just in case the *Star Turn* cameras came by after dawn, to film the jostling queues outside the hotel. They always film the whole audition process, and part of that means gliding by the hordes of losers outside. Getting them to sing and to shout out.

'We have to be ready!' Mam urged us. 'We have to be ready to shine! It could happen any time! But we have to be prepared for the cameras!'

The mother next to us in the queue was nodding and agreeing with her, and shaking her snotty little son awake. Our Eunice started snoring. Mam was close to despair.

'You stay awake, Helen!' she yelled at me. 'You won't let your mam down, will you?'

'No, Mam,' I sighed.

'Just imagine,' Mam said, lowering her voice, so the nosy woman in front of us and the nosy family

4

behind wouldn't hear. 'There'll be no more standing about on the pavement when you've made it. There'll be none of this queueing up with all these untalented drongos then! When you've made it – you and Eunice – we'll be driven everywhere! We'll be flown about the place in a helicopter! We'll live in a huge palace in the countryside and we'll keep everyone waiting! We'll turn up by helicopter, just five minutes before the concert is due to start. Yes! They'll dance to *our* tune then. That's what they'll do.'

Here was Mam, going off on one of her rants again. She knew other people – strangers – were listening. They even gave her a little round of applause afterwards. They liked the sound of what she was saying. They wanted *their* kids to be *discovered* too.

Really, that's what everyone wants, isn't it? To be *discovered*? To become a star, and get that palace in the countryside, and go whizzing about in a helicopter.

Everyone wants to win *Star Turn*.

Except me. I couldn't care less. Not one bit!

I'm having a look around the queue, as the sky gets lighter and lighter and I think: no one would believe me if I said. They wouldn't be able to credit such a thing. Look! Here's a girl who doesn't care

5

about being a star! She doesn't care one jot! What's wrong with her? What's the matter with her?

Mam and Eunice don't believe me. They think I'm weird.

'You've GOT to want to be famous!' Mam shrieks at me. 'You've just GOT to! Listen to your voice! You're like a little angel, Helen! You've got the voice of an angel!'

'I know, I know,' I shrug. Well, it's true. I've got a pure, strong voice. The best in our school. Everyone knows it.

'You can't squander a gift like that,' Mam always warns me. 'You can't just throw it away on some rubbishy career. You have to sing! You have to perform! You have to get out there and give your all!'

'I don't have to if I don't want to.'

'Yes, you do! It's your duty!'

'No, it isn't. Anyway, I want to be a travel agent.'

'No, you don't! Don't be ridiculous, girl! Who on earth wants to be a travel agent?'

'I do! I want to sit at a desk with loads of brochures, all full of pictures of lovely destinations. I want to get on the phone and book flights and hotels for people. I want to help them to have a lovely holiday.'

'Rubbish!' Mam shrieks, just about tearing her hair out. 'You're going to be a star, Helen! You see if you aren't!'

'No,' I said. 'I'm going to be a travel agent, and work in the town centre.'

'Naaagggghhhh!' Mam would shriek. 'You want a palace! You want a helicopter! You want to be on the telly!'

I would shake my head. 'Nonononono!'

This was our usual argument. Sometimes it would go on for days.

Eunice never got involved. You see, Eunice was the apple of Mam's eye. She went along with everything Mam said.

Eunice wanted nothing more than to be a star. With all her heart.

There were songs through the dawn. As the sun came up over the pointed rooftops of the city centre, the queue outside the hotel started singing together. They sounded tired and awful, but everyone joined in. Mam shook Eunice awake and made her join in with the endless, awful medley of popular hits. She jabbed me with her elbows to make me sing. I kept my voice down. I didn't want to show off with the rest of them. Not before I had to. I made the excuse that I was saving my voice.

I was keeping it hidden, like a secret weapon. Mam nodded, approving of that. So I only murmured along, through the early hours of that Saturday. Everyone else was bellowing. It was terrible! I kept thinking about the people trying to sleep in that hotel. What would they think?

But they would know. They would understand. *Star Turn* was one of the most famous shows on TV. Of course they would know why all these people were queueing up outside and moaning their way through a selection of popular chart-toppers. A few faces appeared at dark windows, peering down at us.

And then came the cameras! 'Smile, everyone!' Suddenly everyone in the queue was on their feet. Sleeping bags were rolled up and stowed away. People started doing their hair, spraying themselves with lacquer and smearing make-up on. Vans went by with camera equipment hanging out of the windows and we all had to wave and cheer and grin like maniacs. 'Show that you're enjoying it! Let's see how excited you are!'

The whole thing was a nightmare. I was knackered and wanting a wee. Eunice was dropping asleep again. Mam was beside herself with gibbering excitement. And I knew that it was the kind of excitement that could easily tip over into temper and fury and tears. *Star Turn?* When it came to my mam, *Funny Turn* was more like it.

'We *have* to win' was her mantra. She was muttering it to herself for hours that morning. 'We deserve to win. We *have* to win.'

The woman ahead of us in the queue turned to smile. 'Ah, but it's nice if they get through to the next round, isn't it? That's enough for us. And the taking part. And the atmosphere here. It's enough for us just to be here.' She patted the head of her horrible little brat and grinned at us.

'What?' Mam looked at the woman as if she was crazy. 'No! Don't be ridiculous! We have to win! That's all that matters! Win-win-winning! And being a star!'

'Well,' said the woman, nodding at Eunice, fast asleep on the ground. 'You'll have to wake her up first, won't you? There's only an hour before the doors open.'

Mam cried out and kicked the case Eunice was lying on. Making a disgrace of herself! Showing us up!

'And this one,' the mother in front of us said, gesturing towards me. I scowled up at her. 'Is this one auditioning, too?'

'Of course!' Mam said, scandalised. 'Why ever not? Why shouldn't she?'

'Oh ... er. No reason,' said the woman. 'No reason at all!'

I glared at her until she turned away. Her and her snotty little kid.

I know why the woman asked that, though.

It didn't hurt my feelings, even though Mam thought it must have. Mam hugged me awkwardly. She doesn't give hugs very often. Only when she thinks we must be upset over an audition or an insult. I wriggled out of this one. 'I don't mind,' I said. 'She can say what she wants.' I shrugged. What did I care, if some scraggy old woman looked at me funny and didn't think I should be auditioning? She looked amazed that I would even try to get onto *Star Turn*.

'Some people are so rude,' Mam hissed.

'I don't mind,' I said. 'I don't really want to get on anyway. I'm only here because you made me come along.'

'Don't start arguing again, Helen,' Mam warned, and straightened up. She started peering around, to see where the TV cameras were. They were interviewing losers up near the front of the queue. Mam was ready to dash out and grab their attention, the moment they came anywhere near us. 'You're going to make it, you are,' she warned me. 'Both you

10

and your sister. You're going to get recognised and you're going to make millions and our life will be easy after that. If not at this audition, the next one. And if not then, the one after. But some time soon! It has to happen! It just has to!'

Chapter Two

'Eunice is the talented one. She's the one destined to be the star. Not the youngest one. Not Helen. Oh dear, no. Not Helen.'

I've lived with this all my life. Relatives saying it over my head, thinking I can't hear what they're telling Mam. Neighbours saying it over the garden fence. 'Oh yes. I can see your Eunice being famous. Oh, easily. She's so beautiful. Look at her dancing! Look at her go! Why, she can do anything. You must be so proud of her, Mrs Gutteridge. And, you, Helen. You must be proud of your big sister. Isn't she lovely? Isn't she elegant?'

All my aunties, all the neighbours, all my mam's friends. All of them have said things like this for as long as I can remember. Eunice doing some stupid dance routine for them and grinning and flicking her hair about while I'm getting my head patted and someone's saying: 'You are so lucky to have someone like Eunice in your family.'

Lucky!

She's two years older than me. She's tall and slender and she's pretty, I suppose, to anyone who doesn't really know her. She has all this long golden hair, right down to her bum. She has a pert little nose. Big blue eyes. She looks like no one else in our family.

'Where did you come from, eh?' Mam would laugh and tickle her. 'You're an angel, you are. You're the special one. It must have been your dad's genes. It must be him with all the looks in the family.'

Different dads, you see. Me and Eunice. You couldn't get much more different.

I'm like my mam. On that side of the family, we are plump and short and dark-haired. I'm even shorter and plumper than anyone. I'm a midget, is what Eunice says.

Actually, she says much worse than that. She says I look like a troll. She says I look *squished*.

I'm three feet tall. Officially a dwarf, Mam says.

'But never mind,' she adds brightly. 'It can be your gimmick! Everyone needs a gimmick in showbiz!'

'Yeah,' I scowl. 'The singing dwarf. Great.'

Eunice grins at this. She looks like she's trying to cheer me up. She looks like she's giving a smile

13

of sisterly support. That's how she looks in front of Mam. But I know what Eunice is really like. She gets up in the night to pinch me and twist my arm behind my back. She tortures me nearly all the time. And no one knows about that. No one cares. She looks like an angel, so no one supposes she can misbehave.

But she does. Because she's jealous of me.

Not of my hair, which never does what I want it to. Not of my teeth, which are a bit uneven. Not of my figure, which is dumpy.

Why would Eunice be jealous of me? She's got wonderful looks and hair and skinny hips and she can even hold up a boob tube.

So why *would* Eunice be jealous of me?

Oh yes. It's because of her singing voice.

She sings like a warthog, you see. A growling, snuffling, pig-like warthog. A warthog that has something awful wrong with it. That's how she sounds when she opens her mouth. She wants to sing huge diva-style power ballads, with her voice all soaring and her arms flung wide. And what comes out is monstrous! Atrocious! Grunt – snuffle – warble – grunt grunt grunt!

These audition days are so boring. We've been doing them for four years now, since I was eight.

14

Back then, when I was little – or *littler*, I should say – I thought this was a normal way to carry on: sitting in a hotel foyer with hundreds of other people. Putting on spangly wigs and shimmery costumes. Warming up your voice by going 'LALALALALALAAAA!' and 'MEMEMEME-MEMEMEEEEEE!'

'Louder, girls!' Mam would say. 'Sing out! Sing loud! You've got to do a better warm-up than everyone else! Make the TV cameras come over! They have to let you go through to Round Two if they come and film you! So come on! Sing out!'

Me and Eunice stand there, going 'MEMEME-MEMEEEEEE!' And the cameras hardly ever come our way.

For some reason, we've never got through to the second round. Not in any of the competitions. *Search for a Celeb! Diva Wars! Pop Sensation!* We've auditioned for every single one of those shows. Mam keeps her ear to the ground and watches the local news to see when one of these shows is about to turn up in our town. Other times, we've taken a National Express coach through the night, to some other horrible city we haven't been to before, and we've auditioned there, as well. Just to give us another chance.

15

'LALALALALAAAAAAA! MEMEMEME-
MEMEEEEEEE!'

Everyone warms up at the same time. It's a horrendous noise. People are jumping up and down and squealing with excitement. Some are practising dance moves, or doing the splits.

The main thing about this showbusiness lark is that it's embarrassing.

That particular Saturday, as we were sitting in the foyer and going 'LALALALAAAAA' we were at last noticed by the TV crew. Mam screamed and warned us that they were on the way. 'Oh my god, oh my god,' she panicked, yanking a hair-brush out of her bag. She attacked my knotty, tatty hair, which made me stop singing and start squawking. I was trying to fight her off as the TV presenter came over with a cameraman and sound man. 'OOOwwwwwWWWW, Mam!' I was yelling. 'Leave me alone!'

Eunice was simpering beside us, looking perfect. Looking angelic. 'MEMEMEMEMEMEEEEE!' she grunted, in her best warthog voice. '*KOF KOF KOF*,' she added. Our Eunice always starts coughing when she's nervous. It makes her sound even more like a warthog.

The TV presenter wrinkled his nose. He wasn't sure about interviewing us now. I stopped wriggling in Mam's grasp and stared at him. He was a kids' TV favourite: all dark and good-looking. He was really famous and he'd come over to talk to us! My jaw dropped open. Eunice carried on simpering at him.

'Do you . . . do you mind if we . . . um, interviewed you?' he asked. I was trying to remember his name. Wow! He was hot!

'No, not at all,' Mam said. 'But don't talk to this one.' She glared at me. 'She won't even comb her hair for national TV. Fifteen million people will be watching this, Helen! And you'll be there with your hair stood on end, like a pigging monkey!'

Eunice went on simpering at the sexy boy presenter. Robin! That was it! Robin – he used to be in a dead soppy, awful boyband, until he left and became a presenter. I loved him! He was gorgeous! But I went on scowling at him anyway.

Mam just about grabbed the mike out of his hands. 'Well, Robin. I think my girls really deserve to get through to the final and to win *Star Turn*. They have such amazing talent, both of them. And it hasn't been easy, you know. Bringing them up by myself. We've had some hard times together, me and my girls. But I've promised them. I've said, "Now, girls – talent like yours can't go unnoticed. It can't go unrewarded. You'll see. You'll have the life that I never could have had. You'll both be famous and rich! One day very soon! You'll see! Before you're even fifteen! And we'll live in a palace in the country and have security cameras, all that. We'll whizz about in a helicopter.'"

'Erm, yes,' said Robin, looking a bit flustered.

I really hoped Mam wasn't going into one of her funny turns. She gets herself so worked up. And then it all ends in tears. She opened her mouth again, but Robin managed to break in: 'But do you think your daughters will get through to Round Two?'

'Round Two?' Mam shrieked. 'Round Two?! Of *course* they will! What an insult! Round Two, indeed!'

It was after four in the afternoon before it was our turn.

We had to go and wait on stiff-backed chairs in another corridor with some others. They gave us all numbers and we had to go into a conference room one at a time. The room was soundproofed, so you couldn't hear anything of the auditions inside.

'MEMEMEMEMEEEEEE! *KOF KOF*,' grunted Eunice nervously. Mam jabbed her with an elbow. 'You've warmed up enough now.' Mam was more nervous than I'd ever seen her at one of these things. I think it was because she had given that interview. She had sounded so sure of our success.

We watched others come and go. The cameras and Robin were there to catch them as they came out of the soundproofed audition room.

Some came out wailing and crying and gnashing their teeth. They would fall sobbing into the arms of their mothers and their friends. 'I didn't get in! They said I was rubbish! They said I was wasting their time!'

'Ha!' Mam said, too loudly.

Everyone looked at her. She looked down and pretended to be laughing at something in her magazine. But she kept doing it. She laughed out loud at everyone who came out of the audition room crying. 'HAHAHAHA!' she went. 'Serves them right!'

This only made me and Eunice more nervous. We glanced at each other. It was almost our turns. I was nine hundred and seventy-six and Eunice was nine hundred and seventy-five. She was before me.

What made us even more nervous were the ones who burst out of the audition room screaming and shouting and grinning with delight. With triumph! Flinging their arms around their family and friends

19

and jumping up and down. 'I've made it! I'm through! I'm in the next round!'

'Huh,' Mam would mutter at this lot. 'I bet they can't sing a note. Anyway, they're plug-ugly. They won't get any further than Round Two.' Again, she said it too loudly. But the people who'd succeeded didn't care. They went skipping down the corridor, shrieking with laughter.

'I have every faith in my girls,' Mam said determinedly, grabbing Robin's microphone when he strayed too close. She stared down the camera lens. 'My two girls are bursting with talent! They've got more talent than anyone here! And we've had such a hard life. We've struggled so hard. Both their fathers abandoned us. We've got nothing! Nothing! Just a hope . . . a dream of stardom . . . and glitter running through our showbiz veins.'

Then nine hundred and seventy-five was called in. Eunice got up. She looked like she wanted to cry. When she went walking in through the double doors she was knock-kneed, like she was wetting herself. The doors thudded shut behind her.

Mam started praying.

Ninety seconds later Eunice came back out. Mam jumped up. She ran to her and smothered her oldest daughter to her bosom. 'Well? Well, Eunice?' Mam cried, fully aware of the cameras on her.

'Number nine hundred and seventy-six!' some-one called. My go. I got up.

'I was useless!' Eunice howled. 'I was hopeless! I was rubbish! *KOF! KOF!* Just like I always am!'

'There, there, there, my pet,' Mam was gabbling, covering her with kisses. 'My angel! You're perfect! There, there, there! What do they know, anyway? What do they know about anything?'

I left them to it. Now it was my turn. I took a deep breath. Now that I was here I might as well go for it. For Mam's sake, more than mine. So I was ready. Ready to barge my way into the audition room. Ready to stride across the dark space, to the spot in front of the judges' table. Ready to look all three judges right in the eye. Ready to give them my all.

But what was the point?

I already knew what was going to happen. The same thing that always happened.

Why should this time be any different?

Chapter Three

We didn't take a taxi home that night. We had spent enough taking one there in the first place. 'We don't want to throw good money after bad,' Mam said. So, we gathered together all our showbiz stuff and went to catch a bus in the city centre. Before we left, Mam tried to get us on camera again, telling the world that we would be back: it hadn't seen the last of her beautiful and talented daughters yet.

'Oh, Mam, come on,' Eunice said wearily. 'Let's just go home.'

We didn't even wait around to change out of our glitzy showbiz outfits. Eunice and I stomped across the city centre all dolled up like idiots. But we didn't care by then. Nothing could be more embarrassing than what we had already gone through.

Funny thing was, in the dank, petroly bus station, there were other disappointed people in showbiz outfits, too. I recognised a few faces, puffy with tears. I recognised a few of the parents, too, giving pep talks to their loser children. 'We'll do it next time. The next show that holds auditions. We'll make it! You'll see!'

Mam didn't give Eunice and me a pep talk. She slumped on a plastic bench. All the life had gone out of her. Eunice and I sat either side of her, with all our bags, and waited for our bus.

'They build up your hopes,' Mam said faintly. 'They make it seem so easy. So possible. It just isn't fair.'

At one point, that woman from ahead of us in the morning's queue came past with her snotty son in tow. 'No luck for your two, either?' she said brightly. 'Nigel failed, too. Never mind! There's always next time!'

Mam actually growled at her until she went away, off to her own bus queue.

When our bus eventually came it was very full. It was the time of day when most of the city-centre shoppers returned home with all their carrier bags and parcels. We were cramped up at the back, keeping tight hold of all our stuff.

'What went wrong?' Mam asked at last, as the bus wound its way through the darkening city; through glowing streets of takeaways and leafy suburbs. 'Eunice has told me what went on in her audition. But what about you, Helen? You haven't told me what they said to you.'

I sighed. The truth was, she hadn't asked. She and Eunice had taken one look at my face when I came out of that room, and it had been time to go.

'It was the same as usual,' I said. It was frightening, being so small, standing in the gangway, clutching cases; everyone standing around me, strap-hanging and being jostled as the bus veered around corners. 'They said I sang beautifully. They said that mine was the best voice they had heard all day.'

Mam and Eunice goggled at me. 'And so?' Mam prompted. 'Why couldn't they have let you go through to Round Two? What went wrong?'

I blushed. 'Oh, you know. They *hmmed* and *hahed*, and they looked embarrassed. The fat one in charge talked a lot. Then the skinny woman who used to be a singer talked a lot more about showbusiness. And then the one who is a record producer said a word or two and he was shrugging the whole time. What it all boiled down to was that I don't look right. They said that, to get on in their world, you have to look exactly right. And I don't.'

Mam looked furious at this. So did our Eunice. When I had finished, my sister burst out: 'But *I* look right! I look exactly right! Why couldn't they

24

have taken me? Why didn't they see that I'm exactly what they're after?'

'She is!' Mam added. 'If that's the most important thing, how come they didn't discover Eunice today? She was the most beautiful of all those girls in that place today! By a long way! She always is! What's *wrong* with them? Why haven't they discovered her yet?'

'I don't know,' I said, in a quiet voice. 'I didn't think they looked very clever, though, that panel. Remember last year? Remember the kinds of people who won through last year? Drongos! Losers! Nitwits!' I laughed, trying to cheer the two of them up.

'I don't care about other people,' Mam said. 'I just wish *we* could win through. Just once. I wish we could win just anything.'

I peered through the forest of legs and bums and Argos bags, through the dark windows, and realised that the bus was slowing at our stop. 'This is us!' I cried out, trying to rouse Mam and Eunice from their defeated stupor.

We hadn't been in our new house for long. This part of the city and this estate was still pretty new to us, and we didn't know our way around that well. For a second, as we stood on the pavement with our make-up cases and bags of outfits, I thought we had got off at the wrong place, and an awful feeling of lostness came over me. But it was okay. We were home. Mam sighed and led the way to our house.

We live in a long terrace, near the grocer's and the betting shop. Our estate was pretty quiet that night. Luckily we didn't know any of our neighbours yet, so we didn't have to tell anyone how we had failed.

Eunice was checking her watch as Mam unlocked the back door. 'Legend Hunt is on in a few minutes,' she said. 'Then it's Search for a Celeb.' She was trying to get her enthusiasm back, I could see.

'I don't care,' Mam grunted, shunting the door open. 'Just dump everything in the hallway. We'll put it all away tomorrow. I want a pizza and I want a gin and tonic. Come on, girls! Action! Helen, fetch out the takeaway menus! Eunice, pour me a drink!'

Mam went into the living room and flung herself down on the sofa. She had a battle of wills first with Mr Rancid, our adopted cat, who was sitting in her favourite place. He spat and hissed and slunk away. He knew he wouldn't get anywhere in a fight with Mam. Not when she was in this mood.

Eunice and I were tiptoeing around her. We knew she was liable to explode at any moment.

26

'Here's your drink, Mam!'

'Do you need headache pills?'

'I've phoned for two twelve-inch Hawaiians!'

The telly came bursting on, into light and noise and colour. Contestants were prancing about under neon lights. They were singing their hearts out. Sweating and contorting their faces. They were giving it their all for the judges on *Legend Hunt*. The judges sat back and judged solemnly. They frowned and concentrated and took their judging very seriously.

'I hate them! I hate them all!' Mam cried out at last, passing her glass to Eunice for a refill. Eunice hurried over to the sideboard. 'What do they know? What makes them experts? What do the judges know about my girls and what we have gone through? And how much they deserve stardom, eh? What do they know about anything?'

Her voice was going shrill. 'Mam,' I said. 'There's no point in yelling at the telly.'

Mistake. She swung round on me. 'Oh, there isn't, is there, madam? Is that a fact?'

There was a knock at the back door. Our pizza delivery. Eunice went dashing for it, glad to get away.

'I'll tell you something, little lady,' Mam snarled at me. 'You should be glad that your mother is

27

sticking up for you! That she believes in you! Why, my mother didn't bother with me at all! Not in the slightest! She never wanted me to succeed, to make something of myself! And look at me! Dragging you two round all over the place! Pushing you on, to do better things! To be stars!'

I looked away. I urged Eunice to hurry up and bring our pizzas and distract Mam from her ranting.

'But, you!' Mam cried. 'You can't make the effort, can you? You can't even comb your hair down before your audition. Or, if you do, it comes springing up again, just to spite me! I put lovely clothes on you. I spend all my money on buying smashing outfits for you. And you look terrible in them! They're all creased and splattered with food after about five minutes! You go into auditions looking just awful, Helen. That's why you never get through. And I think you do it just to spite me, don't you? Just to torture your mam?'

At that moment – at last – Eunice came through with the pizzas. She was simpering and striding about with the boxes. There was a delicious scent of ham and cheese and pineapple.

'Look at your sister!' Mam shrieked. 'She tries! She tries her hardest! She looks every inch a star when she goes into an audition!' Then she glared savagely at Eunice. 'What's that you've got there?'

'P-pizza . . .'

'Pizza? Who ordered pizza?'

'Y-you told us to phone—'

'We can't afford phone-up pizzas! We've already spent a fortune today!' Mam jumped up off the settee. 'Give me those!' She grabbed the hot, flat boxes out of Eunice's hands and pulled them off her. 'And you two can't afford to go eating fattening muck like this. You have to work to maintain your figure as it is, Eunice. You can't start pigging out now! And you, Helen – you don't want to be a fat dwarf! Don't eat filth!'

With that, Mam stormed past us, narrowly missed stepping on Mr Rancid, and barged her way into the kitchen. We heard her yelling after the pizza man, but he had already disappeared into the night. 'Gaaaggghhh!' Mam yelled out into the night sky, and that awful screech summed up all of the day's frustration and pent-up fury. We hurried to her, just in time to see her sling the pizzas into our muddy garden. They landed with a cheesy splat.

Mam slammed the kitchen door and rounded on the two of us. 'If you two were as bothered about making a success of your lives as you were about ordering rubbishy food—!' Then she stopped, abruptly. She sagged down and started to cry.

'Bedtime, Mam,' our Eunice said. 'It's been a long day.'

We both helped her upstairs. It was a bit of an assault course, getting her down the hallway and up the stairs. We still hadn't unpacked our things properly, into the new place. There were cardboard boxes and tea chests everywhere. Mam kept banging bits of herself against all the sharp corners. At last though, she fell into her bed and lay still. The curtains were still drawn from this morning, when she had risen in the middle of the night, full of excitement about the auditions.

'She's so disappointed,' Eunice said quietly, as we stood in the doorway and listened to her breathing. 'Is she lying okay, do you think? What if she throws up in her sleep?'

'I think she's okay.' I frowned. 'Let's leave her sleeping.' My stomach was growling really loudly. I was starving!

'She'll be up at the crack of dawn again,' Eunice sighed.

'Oh no! Why?'

'Car bootie, remember. Over in Denton. She's put the money down for a table-top. We'll have to go with her.'

'I suppose so.' In recent months Mam had become addicted to car booties and table-top sales.

She would suddenly announce that it was time we got rid of all of our unwanted junk. We all had to bring out our stuff and donate it to the cause. Any profits would go into our showbiz fund for costumes, make-up, taxi fares. The thing was, Mam kept being tempted by all sorts of things when we were out at these sales. She loved old ornaments. China ladies. Porcelain kittens. We ended up coming back with nearly as much junk as we started out with.

She wouldn't be dissuaded though. Sunday morning was car-boot morning and, hungover or not, she would be raring to go. And we would have to be there too.

I put it out of my mind and raced downstairs.

'You're not going to rescue the pizzas . . .' Eunice said, screwing up her face. 'Oh, how degrading!'

Eunice can be proper hoity-toity when she wants.

'Of course I am!' I put the kitchen lights on, and tried to see by their glare as I tiptoed down the muddy garden. Both pizzas had landed reasonably safely. The lids had flown open and steam was coming off them, into the night air. Luckily they hadn't landed in the mud or cat poo or whatever. I reckoned they were okay to eat. I looked back at the house and gave Eunice the thumbs up. She tutted, but I knew she was dead hungry, too.

Poor Mam, I thought, looking up at her window. We should put a cold slice or two on her bedside table, in case she woke in the night.

As I bent to pick the pizzas up, I remembered a fairy tale I used to read in some old book I had when I was a little kid. Something about the mother chucking something out of the kitchen window and yelling at her kid. That was it: magic beans. The beanstalk. 'What have you brought, Jack? What are these supposed to be?' But that night the beanstalk started to grow . . .

I looked at the pizzas lying in the weeds in our garden and imagined cheesy tendrils lifting up and growing into the sky. Higher and higher, all covered in bits of pineapple and ham. A huge great pizza beanstalk going up, up, up into the land of fame.

Chapter Four

That Sunday turned out to be a lucky one. It was the day that Mam met Eric.

Not that that meant all our troubles were over. Not by a long chalk. I mean, Eric wasn't a showbiz agent, or a record producer or anything, though he did like to say he was in the music business. Nor was he a millionaire, either. He wouldn't have been flogging things at Denton car bootie if he'd had millions, would he?

But Eric was a nice bloke. And that Sunday was the day he met Mam.

He had set up his stall next to hers and at first she was cross because he was too noisy. He was yelling about what CDs he was selling. He had the loudest voice you've ever heard. 'I've got disco! Classical! Rock 'n' roll! All the lovely old show tunes!'

Mam was slumped over the table where we had laid out our fluffy toys, old ornaments, comics and books. That morning she was looking slightly grey and she hadn't had time to wash her hair. 'Can't anyone tell that man to quieten down?' she groaned.

'I've got world music! Cajun! Polka! Japanese! I've got medieval monks chanting and hip-hop!'

Eric was a plump man, fairly young. Probably about the same age as Mam. He was wearing a T-shirt that had the name of some old band on it, and his baseball cap was on back to front. He was grinning away and shouting out, as if it didn't matter to him that none of the people drifting by stopped and took a look at his wares. He had boxes and boxes of CDs laid out and, from the sound of it, he had every kind of music going.

'Heavy metal! Opera! Motown! Come and have a flick through my CDs! You're sure to find something you've always wanted!'

Mam was groaning. 'Oh, we should never have come out today. Not after all the humiliation of yesterday.'

What was she on about? It was our humiliation, not hers. She hadn't been the one getting rejected.

'Go and get me some bottled water or something, will you, Eunice?' Mam said pitifully. 'I don't know why I'm so dehydrated. It must be all the excitement from yesterday.'

Eunice took her spare change and dashed off.

I was left to watch our stall of junk, while Mam slumped in her deckchair.

'I can't even be bothered having a walk round and seeing what's for sale,' she said. 'I must really be sickening for something.'

Ours was a very unpopular corner of the car-boot sale. We were having as few people stop by as Eric at the next stall.

'Slow morning, eh?' he grinned over, at one point.

'What did that man say?' Mam sat upright. 'Was he talking to us?'

I nodded.

Mam glared at him. 'He's an oaf.'

'Glam rock!' Eric was bellowing. 'Folk music! Europop!'

'Tell him to pipe down, Helen,' Mam groaned. 'Otherwise I'm going to get up and smack him one.'

I went over and repeated this, and Eric laughed loudly. 'Bit hungover, is she? Oh dear!'

Mam overheard this. 'I am not! What is she saying to you? Little madam! How dare you!' Mam yanked off her designer sunglasses and jumped up.

'Hello,' Eric said. 'I'm Eric.'

'So?' said Mam. She glared suspiciously at all of his golden chains and bracelets. He had a gold necklace with his name on. He had rings on every finger. Mam hated bling. She thought it was common. I watched her toss her long hair in contempt. 'Well, *Eric*, maybe you could just shut the hell up for a bit? I've had enough of your inane hectoring for one morning.' She sat down again and put her sunglasses back on. They looked posh, but I knew she'd got them free out of a magazine.

'Your mam's gorgeous,' Eric told me. 'Is she always as rude as that, though?'

'She is,' I said, flicking through his blues CDs.

'Hmm,' said Eric, staring at her, and just about rubbing his hands with glee. 'I think she'd be in with a chance with me, if she was a bit less rude and nasty.'

I giggled at this.

'No, it's true,' Eric went on. 'She's a good-looking woman, your ma. But she spoils herself, doesn't she? Being a bit horrible and all.'

I could see that Mam was biting her tongue and pretending not to listen. He was winding her right up!

'Ah, well,' Eric said. 'I reckon she's missed out. She's missed her chance with me, I think. I don't like women who shout.' He smiled at me. 'What do they call you, then?'

I blinked up at him. He seemed to be miles tall, silhouetted against the sun. 'I'm Helen. My sister –

who's just gone off – she's Eunice. My mam's name is—'

'Well, I'm not so bothered about that now.'

I watched Mam purse her lips crossly. She yanked a magazine off her table sale and flicked through it savagely.

'How much are your CDs?' I asked him.

'Everything's a pound,' he said. 'Because I don't like doing sums much.'

I nodded. 'I hate sums, too.'

'Are you a dwarf, then?' he asked.

I glared up at him. I couldn't believe it! No one ever asked that. No adult, anyway. They hedged around the subject. They would never bring it up willingly. They just patronised me and patted me on the head and treated me in a way they thought was nice. But Eric had just come straight out and asked me! Not nastily, or like he was making fun of me. He was really interested. He was peering down at me and staring like he would if he was in the jungle and came across some creature he'd never seen before. Like a marmoset or a tapir.

'Yes,' I said. 'I am.'

He nodded happily. 'Thought so. Funny-looking thing, aren't you? Nothing like your sister.'

Again, I stared at him, amazed. No one I knew talked like this. It was like he said whatever came into his mind. I coughed. 'Well, Eunice is the pretty one. She's the one who's going to be a star.'

'Oh? Why's that?'

'Um. Well. She's very pretty and slim.'

Eric frowned. 'She's got bandy legs, though.'

'What?!' I had never, ever heard anyone criticise anything about Eunice's appearance. It had simply never happened before.

'It's true!' he laughed. 'She's got skinny legs, and they're just a bit bandy.'

Mam threw off her sunglasses again. 'I don't know who you think you are!' she screeched at Eric. 'But how *dare* you say these horrible things about my daughters! Calling her a dwarf! Saying our Eunice is bandy!'

Eric shrugged. 'Hey, your mother's talking to us again.'

'You are an impertinent, fat and sweaty man!' Mam shouted. Her insulting him was pretty lame, actually. Eric looked like he didn't care what anyone called him.

'What kind of star are you going to be, then?' he asked me.

'Me?' I said, and hurriedly went back to checking out his CDs. I was on the glam rock section now. I love that era of music. All the silly clothes: satin and sparkles, moon boots and leopard skin.

Fantastic! 'I'm not going to be any kind of star. I've given up trying.'

'What?' Mam shouted. 'What did you say, Helen? You've got the voice of an angel! You can't let it go to waste!'

I shook my head, laughing. I was enjoying myself now. Eric and his rudeness, his whole weird way of talking, had cheered me up. The sun had broken through the heavy clouds and from the burger van there was this terrific smell of frying onions.

'So!' Eric said. 'You're a singer, are you?'

'Not really.' Wow – a pound each for these CDs! He had some great obscure ones by glam stars from over thirty years ago. Brilliant records that I knew from the radio! And even older ones by fabulous diva-type singers who wore daring evening dresses and belted out these huge numbers. I loved seeing clips of these old stars on the telly. I'd think: that's when stars were real stars. Not like now. And Eric had them all for sale – so cheaply – on his stall. I'd end up spending all my cash on CDs at this rate.

Eric was putting a CD in his clunky silver machine and cranking up the speakers. 'Come on then, Helen. Let's hear you.'

I looked up, squinting against the sun. My heart skipped a beat then, because he had plugged a cheap microphone into his machine. Now he was holding it out to me. 'Come on then. If you're as good as your mam reckons. Let's be hearing you.'

Eric was a sharp one. He had noticed the kind of music I'd been looking at in his collection. He had found the right karaoke track for me. I recognised it at once: some ancient silly singalong number; all summery and shivery with a belting chorus. I knew it off by heart.

'Come on, then!' He lifted a whole load of junk off one of his tables and made me an impromptu stage. Before I could even open my mouth to protest, he had picked me up like a doll and set me up on this podium in the middle of his record stall.

I froze with shock. Mam was staring at me, getting to her feet. Eric was beginning to clap. Our Eunice was just coming back with the water. And then the song kicked in. 'Alligator Disco Stomp'. A fantastic glam classic from 1974. Right. I'd show them.

And I started to sing.

'Huh,' Eunice said. 'It wasn't so great.'

'Yes, it was!' Mam beamed. 'She was fantastic! She was a glam-rock genius!'

I glowed with pleasure at this.

It was a couple of hours after my triumph at the car-boot sale. We were sitting in a greasy café at the other end of the car park. We were having Welsh rarebit and baked beans for our Sunday lunch and great big mugs of sugary tea. Food had never tasted so great! I was so worked up and excited still, after the show I'd put on at Eric's stall. I ate with great gusto, and grinned at my mam, who was grinning back at me. She was actually proud of me! She was looking at me like I was the most brilliant and talented daughter in the world.

'I think she made a show of herself,' Eunice said miserably, cutting her cheese-on-toast into smaller and smaller pieces. She looked totally depressed.

'She did not!' Mam cried. 'Everyone thought she was absolutely marvellous!'

That was the thing. That's what clinched it. That's what gave me the biggest buzz of all: a crowd had gathered around me as I stood there on Eric's table-top. Within minutes a whole gaggle of car-boot people were clapping and swaying along and cheering between songs.

That's right. *Songs* plural. Because, as soon as 'Alligator Disco Stomp' had crashed to an amazing finish, we were straight onto another fave track, and then another. Eric was my musical arranger, flicking the karaoke CD to song after song, and somehow – I don't know how – each song he chose was one that I loved. I ended up doing practically a whole concert there, for the crowd that was gathering. Eric was clapping along, and so was Mam. Mam's face had been shining with pride. Eric looked delighted because some of the people there were starting to flick through his CDs. Suddenly he had customers!

'Who'd have thought it?' Mam laughed, slurping her tea happily. 'That old-fashioned kind of music! That was popular when I was a kid! Who'd have thought you could sing that kind of stuff?'

'Huh,' scowled Eunice, her face dark with anger.

'But it's my favourite!' I said. 'I've tried to tell you, but you never listen. I don't like music that's coming out today. I like older things! Classic things!'

'She's the dancing retro midget,' Eunice sneered.

'I'm going to fetch you such a slap, if you don't stop that,' Mam snapped at her.

Eunice's face fell. 'What?'

'You heard me, madam. Don't you dare try to bring your sister down.'

'But she was like a performing freak! That's how they were treating her!'

'Pssshhaawww!' Mam said fiercely, shushing her. Then she grinned at me again.

I stopped eating. Really? A performing freak? I hadn't thought of that. Is that what that crowd had seen? Me, doing all my stomping and dancing and jitterbugging about on that table-top and singing my heart out. Getting them to wave their arms in the air along with me, and sing along with the chorus. Is that what they had seen? A performing midget? A circus act? I gulped down hard.

'Your sister is just saying horrible things because she's jealous,' Mam told me. 'Take no notice of her.'

Suddenly Eunice said, 'Oh, no! Look what's just come in! We've been followed!'

Sure enough, Eric was stepping into the café. He had finished loading up his car and had popped in to see us. 'To see my star!' he grinned, nudging me as he sat down at our table, pinching a chip from the bowl we were sharing in the middle. 'Wasn't she great, eh?' he said, looking round at my mam and sister. 'Wasn't she just brilliant?'

Chapter Five

One of the best things about Eric, right from the start, was his fearlessness. He would ask questions that I would never dare to. He wasn't like most grown-ups, in the way that you can see them thinking things over, and deciding not to ask or say the obvious thing. Eric would come straight out with it. It was a talent he had. So, the first time he came round our house, he was like: 'Why is there all this rubbish in your garden? What are those pizza boxes lying on the flowerbeds for?' And, when he went inside, he frowned and asked: 'How come half your stuff is still packed in boxes and crates? How can you live like that?'

Mam was gobsmacked by all of this. She had never had anyone questioning her life like this. After about an hour of Eric being round ours she looked like she wished she had never asked him. She was scowling at him across our dinner table. Eunice was scowling at him, too. Eric didn't even notice. He was tucking into his dinner happily and greedily, and looking around him with interest.

We were eating everything-in-the-fridge stew, which was Mam's favourite recipe. 'Oh, you'd never believe how easy it is,' she enthused. 'It's delicious and nutritious. You just get the biggest pan you've got and put it on the hob. Then you open up your fridge and you empty everything from your fridge into the pan. Turn on the heat, and stir. For about three or four hours.'

'Right . . .' said Eric. He looked down at his plate thoughtfully.

'What if there's chocolate bars in your fridge?' I asked.

'They go in as well!'

'And what if there's like . . . a whole jar of Lazy Chilli?'

'All of it has to go in! Every bit! That's the rule. You have to empty your whole fridge, and eat the whole lot.'

'What about your migraine headache cooling gel eyemask?' I asked, trying to catch Mam out. 'Surely you couldn't put that in?'

She tutted at me. 'Well, of course not. Everything else, though. Trifle and fish-fingers and sweet potatoes and honey and pork chops and . . .' She was counting everything off on her fingers and I put down my fork, feeling a bit funny.

'Hmm,' said Eric. 'That's why it tastes like crap.' He put down his knife and fork, beaming at us all.

'WHAT?' I could see that Mam was furious. She wasn't at all charmed by Eric's cheerful honesty. Her thinking was: if she could be arsed to cook a nice big dinner for her family – plus some near-stranger – then the least they could do is enjoy it. Or pretend to enjoy it.

Cue some quality sucking-up opportunity for our Eunice. 'I think it's lovely, Mam. It's the best empty-fridge stew you've ever made for us.'

Mam's face was dark. 'No, it's not. It's diabolical. It's revolting. Stop eating it at once, Eunice! It was a waste of five hours of my life! Eric is right! It's all going in the bin right now!'

'No, no, Mam,' I put in. 'It's okay. We can finish it up . . .' It was at the point where I'd say anything to calm her down. She was veering close to the edge again, standing up and grabbing at our plates.

'No!' she said. 'In the bin with it! It tastes like crap, apparently!'

'Best place for it!' Eric laughed. 'Get it in the bin!' He sat back complacently and fished out his mobile phone, which was dinky and flashy. 'Shall I ring up for a Chinese or summat?'

Mam shrugged bitterly, making her way to the kitchen with the plates. 'Whatever you want, Eric. Just do whatever you want. You're obviously a man who knows his own mind.'

He started tapping in the number of his favourite takeaway. 'All right, I will.'

'I mean, don't think you'll hurt my feelings, or anything.'

'Okay,' he said.

'After you've rejected my food. After humiliating me, in front of my daughters.' Mam was sniffling, all tearful.

Eric looked up from his phone. 'Aren't you being a drama queen!' he said to Mam.

'WHAT?!'

'Aren't you laying it on a bit thick? Trying to make us all feel guilty. What's that for? Why do you want to do that?'

'I beg your pardon?'

He shrugged. 'I just think it's a funny way of carrying on. All this pretending that we've upset you. It's as if you're wallowing in pretend misery. What's that for?'

Mam looked dumbstruck. 'I think I'm getting a migraine,' she said.

'Right, girls! What's your favourite Chinese? Let's get a banquet in, eh?'

He keyed the number in with a flourish. Wowee! I thought. He knows the numbers of takeaways off by heart! He can order them any time of day! Now *that* was something that only a grown-up could do. It made the whole business of growing up seem worthwhile.

You Can Be Mega-Famous! was going to be on that night. It was the quarter-final. It was on quite late, but Mam had promised that we could stay up, even though it was a school night.

We ate everything that Eric had delivered in his banquet and loved every bit of it. By the end he was beaming with satisfaction. 'Best thing is,' he said, 'it's all in paper cartons. No washing up! You can chuck it all away.'

'Is that why you're so fat?' I asked him, toying with my chopsticks. 'Because you eat takeaways all the time?'

Eunice gave a sharp intake of breath. Her eyebrows shot up in alarm. Mam started clearing up the table in embarrassment. 'Helen! Don't be rude! Eric's probably got some kind of glandular disorder or something.'

'Nope,' he said. 'Helen's right. I'm fat because I order in food every night. See that banquet for four on the menu? Well, I can eat a whole banquet

48

for four in one go.' We had ordered the banquet for six, even though there was only four of us and Eunice only ever picks at her food.

'Doesn't that make you feel ill?' I asked.

'Or guilty?' said Mam. 'What with all the starving people in the world?'

Eric rubbed his belly under his tracksuit top. 'No way!' he said. 'It's lush. I love Chinese food! I love Italian food! I love all food, actually. Why should I feel guilty or sick?'

Mam gave him a little smile, but you could see she was disgusted. 'Helen, fetch him another beer out of the fridge. Eric, why don't you settle yourself in front of the telly? The show will be starting soon.'

He lumbered off to make himself comfortable.

I was opening up our fridge – which is hard for me, at my height – when Mam came through with all the crushed-up wrappings and paper cartons and plates. Our fridge was empty apart from the lagers Eric had brought.

Mam said thoughtfully, 'I think he must be a very sad, damaged person really.' She started stuffing rubbish into the bin. 'All that grinning isn't natural. He's nervous, isn't he?' She sighed. 'I suppose I'm a bit fond of him. But he gets on my nerves, really. I should never have invited him round. What do you think, Helen? Do you think he's embarrassing?'

I slammed the fridge shut. 'I think he's great!' Then I went out on a limb. 'I love him!'

Mam burst out laughing at me. 'You can't say that! My god, Helen! He's almost a complete stranger! You can't go round making snap decisions like that. You've got to ... I don't know ... be more careful than that.'

'I think he's fantastic,' I said. 'He made me get up and sing for everyone at the car bootie on Sunday. And he knew just the kind of songs I wanted to sing.'

Mam smiled at me and put the kettle on. Then she poured herself a quick, strong gin. 'But he's a bit on the chunky side. And he's proper cheeky, too. And all of that common jewellery!'

I shrugged. 'I think he's great.'

Eunice came through. 'Mam! He's got the remote control and he's whizzing through all the channels! He's changing all our settings! He's taken the back off the cable TV box thing and is messing about with it. And ... and Mr Rancid went and sat straight on his lap!' Eunice looked like she wanted to spit.

Mam laughed. 'He's certainly making himself at home.'

'I think he's horrible,' Eunice said. 'Vulgar.'

'Now then, Eunice,' Mam said. 'You shouldn't be judgemental about people.'

Eunice looked stung. She hated being told off. She hated to think she was anything less than perfect.

'Are you going to marry him, Mam?' I asked, on my way back to the living room.

'What?!' she laughed.

'I think you should,' I said. And then I went to take him his beer.

'I've improved the telly reception,' he said. 'And found some more channels for you.' Our notoriously unfriendly Mr Rancid really *was* sitting on his lap and letting Eric stroke him. 'Thing is, all the settings have changed now.' Eric went on to explain what he had done to the remote control, and I suddenly realised what he was behaving like tonight.

He was *auditioning* for us. It was no different to us going and queueing up for *Search for a Celeb*, or whatever. He wasn't singing a song or dancing, but Eric was auditioning anyway: for the role of our stand-in dad. Mam's fella. He wanted to be the man of our house.

We watched the show together. There were four acts: a puppeteer, a fire-eater who sang while he ate fire, a knife-throwing act and a huge fat woman who sang opera kind of stuff while walking on a tightrope.

Eric wasn't impressed. 'It's all gimmicks, isn't it?' he sighed. 'It's like the circus.'

'Well,' said Mam. 'You have to have a gimmick. That's what it's all about, these days. There are so many people in showbusiness, trying to make it big. You have to find a way of standing out.'

We all watched the opera singer holding a tiny parasol, warbling in Italian and wobbling along on her pointy feet. It was like she was going to fall at any second. All the audience were holding their breath. Urging her on.

'Fall! Fall!' Eric shouted out. 'Go on! Fall off the rope!'

Eunice glared at him. She couldn't believe his bad taste. She was sitting well away from us, on a dining-room chair she had dragged through. I was sitting on the settee, taking up only a tiny corner, and Eric was spread out on the rest of it. He was shouting out like he was in his own place. Despite what Mam had said, I didn't think he'd been nervous at all tonight. He had carried on like he had known us for years.

Mam was in her favourite armchair, with her legs curled up beneath her. She had unfastened her hair from the 'do it was in, and seemed to feel more comfortable. She kept glancing at Eric over the rim of her tall glass as she sipped. You could see she wasn't very bothered about the outcome of the show. That was unusual for her. She watched these sorts of shows avidly.

'You don't need gimmicks,' Eric was saying. 'Not if you've got real talent.'

'Huh,' Eunice said. 'Like you'd know.'

He just shrugged and laughed.

'Eunice,' Mam said. 'Don't be nasty to our guest.'

Eunice tossed her head. She looked like a pony, snorting like that, with her hair tied up.

'If you've got a good voice,' Eric said, 'you don't need anything else. You just rely on your voice. You don't have to walk a tightrope or breathe fire or show off your boobs.'

We all stared at him. He'd said 'boobs' on our settee! The first time he came round our house!

But our attention was grabbed then, by the telly. And the fact that, just at the crucial moment, the big opera woman's Italian song ended in a horrible gurgling scream. At the very last moment her tiny feet slipped! And she fell off the rope! She plummeted down to the huge pile of mattresses and we watched, holding our breath, along with millions of others, as she bounced and bounced and bounced.

Eventually Eric said: 'Well, I reckon that's won it for her, don't you?'

We all looked at him. 'Huh?'

The poor fat woman was showing all her knickers as she bounced up and down. The audience, seeing that she was safe, started to laugh.

'She's made them feel sorry for her. She's got them on her side. That's all you have to do, you know. To succeed. Make them feel a bit sorry for you . . .'

Chapter Six

Our Eunice doesn't pay much attention to me when we're at school. I think she pretends she isn't even related to me. The girls she hangs around with are tall and pretty like her, and they clip around the place looking all snotty and superior.

That Thursday night I was held back for a bit, because I'd thumped someone in the corridor. I don't know what his name was. Some lad who'd been shoving past me. Anyway, I'd caused a bit of a scrap at hometime and our Eunice had been called back by the deputy head, to see that I got home without causing any more bother.

I was sitting on a chair in the deputy head's office, waiting to be taken home by my older sister. I looked at the family photos on his desk. He had a surprisingly pretty wife and bored-looking kids.

'Mam's gonna kill you,' Eunice said, when she turned up. She was really miffed at being called back. She was mortified at having to leave her gaggle of skinny friends and look after me. She wanted to twist my ear, really hard, and would have done, but the deputy head was standing behind her.

'Helen gets herself overwrought sometimes,' the deputy head fretted to Eunice. 'As a result of her . . . condition.'

'What condition?' I said.

He looked to Eunice for help.

'He means you being a midget,' Eunice sighed.

'Ah, well, that's not *quite* what I meant . . .'

'That's charming!' I said, hopping off the chair and picking up my school bag. 'Yeah, maybe he's right. Maybe I'll have to thump a few more kids, just to help me get over the trauma.'

The deputy head looked weak at this. I was feeling pretty tough just then. And I was looking fierce, too, with my hair all spiked up. My shins and knees were scabby from playing out at lunchtime and I'd put a few holes in my blouse. I was looking wild! And now he was saying, because I was small, I could get away with just about anything! Hurray!

Eunice gave me a simmering look. She was going to clout me once we were outside, I could tell.

'Your sister is having some trouble adjusting to life here at the Mortlake Centre for Excellent Excellence in the Arts and IT (formerly known as Mortlake Comp). Unlike you, Eunice, who have been such a model pupil. A star pupil, in fact.'

Eunice was fluttering her eyelashes at him as he led us out into the main entrance hall. 'Oh well. Helen is very special, in her own way.'

'How long is it you've been with us, girls? Four months? Helen, you should really be settling in by now. You should take a leaf out of your sister's book.'

Huh, yeah, I thought. Take a leaf out of her book, and wipe my bum with it.

'I don't think Helen likes the KOF KOF subjects she has to do here,' Eunice simpered.

'But we have a very broad-based curriculum . . .'

'She wants to be a travel agent,' Eunice said. 'All she wants to learn about is geography and stuff about tickets and reservations.'

'Shut up,' I growled.

'She does geography,' the deputy head said. 'Everyone has to do geography.'

Yeah, but that was just about, like, farming and pigs and industry and all that. It wasn't really about *places*. At least, not as much as it should be.

The deputy head waved us away out of the building. He said he hoped I would develop a better attitude.

Seriously, what's wrong with wanting to be a travel agent?

It's more sensible than wanting to be a star. More likely, too. Even for a midget with a bad attitude. No one goes telling our Eunice she's bound to fail. No one tells *her* she's wasting her time when she practises her dance moves in our bedroom or warbles away into a hairbrush.

All I want to know about is the world.

I've got a globe at home. It's not a marvellous one. It hasn't got all the places on. Just the main ones. And the colours are pretty unrealistic. It's for a little kid, I suppose. But then, I've had it for a few years now. My dad's mam, my grandma, bought it for me when I was tiny. She must have started this whole travel thing off with that present. It's an inflatable globe. It takes ages to blow up, like a big beach ball. I lie in bed with it, going round and round the world: mapping out possible journeys by boat or plane or road. I make lists of destinations in my head: the more exotic and unpronounceable, the better. When Eunice yells at me to turn out the lights so she can get her beauty sleep, I do so. But I get my pen-torch out and that's even better for tracing my way round and round the world. It's like looking at all the places from outer space and deciding where to go first.

Eunice can't see the attraction. 'It's not like you

want to be an air stewardess or anything glamorous, is it?'

'No, I want to be a travel agent. And make up journeys for people and organise things for them.'

'Pah,' Eunice would say. 'You're such a freak, Helen. And Mam's not very happy with you having such mundane ambitions. She's very disappointed by that. She wants her daughters to reach for the stars. *Both* her daughters.' She looked down at me. 'Mind, you'd never get anywhere, obviously.'

By now we had walked all the way down the school drive. We'd walked past all the newly put up signs which said things like: *Working together to create excellent excellence!* and *A partnership in working together! For getting YOU the necessary grades you need!* There were no other kids in sight. Everyone had fled the place as soon as the hometime bells had rung. Most of the teachers had sped past us in their battered old cars, too. Eunice realised that we were alone now, and she looked ready to start up her usual torture; a bit of hair-pulling maybe. Or twisting my arms all the way home.

But then she stopped. 'Oh no,' she cursed.

'What? What is it?' She sounded like she had seen something awful.

There, in the street outside the school gates, was an old red car. I don't know what cars are called, different types and all that. I could tell, though, that this was an old knackered one. It doors were opening and Eric was getting out, with a big daft grin all over his face. And out of the passenger side came our mam, and she was grinning as well.

'What's she doing smiling?' Eunice hissed. 'What's she doing in a nasty old car like that? People will see her! She's showing us up!'

'Girls! You're late!' Mam yelled, waving her arms.

'I was in a fight,' I explained, hurrying over. 'We got held back so the deputy head could have a go at me about being a midget. Anyway, what are you doing in Eric's car? How come you're meeting us from school?'

She grinned. 'Get in! We're going to the shopping mall. It's Eric's idea! It's a surprise.'

Eunice's face was a picture. Her face was like: I'm not getting in *that*.

Eric was flipping the front seats forward so we could climb in the back. His car smelled of smokey bacon crisps, fags and Mam's perfume. 'What do you mean, the deputy head was having a go about you being a midget?'

I hopped in easily onto the back seat. 'Oh, I don't know. Some rubbish he was saying. I can't settle into this school because I'm a midget. He's a bit daft.'

Eunice sighed, and tried to haul herself into the back seat. Her lanky arms and legs were sticking out at all angles. 'That's not exactly what Mr Price was saying, Helen, and you know it. He was simply saying that you are probably maladjusted because of you being stunted and deformed.'

'Stunted and deformed!' Mam cried out. 'Is that what he said?'

'Do you want me to thump him?' Eric said bravely. 'No one insults you girls! You hear that? I'll stick up for you!' He climbed back into his driver's seat, and Mam patted his knee affectionately.

On the back seat, Eunice exchanged a swift glance with me. Mam patted his knee! That could mean only one thing.

Eric drove quite recklessly. It didn't seem altogether dangerous, but I did feel the wheels on the left leave the road at one point, as we bounced off the city ring road and onto the road that would take us to the mall.

'It's late-night closing!' Mam said. 'We can buy some new tops and maybe a skirt or something. Nice things.'

'And,' said Eric. 'There's that special thing happening as well, isn't there?'

'What?' I asked. 'What is it?'

'You'll both find out when we get there.'

It was a lovely, sunny evening, with the sun gleaming on the glass front of the football stadium and the choppy waters of the quay as we zoomed and swerved past. Eric put one of his CDs on – an old Fifties rock 'n' roll compilation. You'd have thought it would be too old for us to know any of those songs, but we did. They soon had all four of us singing along as Eric chivvied his way through the teatime traffic.

'That's right, girls!' he laughed. 'Sing out! Sing loud!'

Eventually we arrived at the huge, glitzy domes and towers of the shopping mall. It was bejewelled like a palace in *The Arabian Nights*. It made me feel dizzy, thinking of all the gorgeous clothes and things inside it. And all the music! Its record stores stocked every single piece of music ever recorded! Just imagine that!

We whizzed around all the levels of the multi-storey, looking for a space.

Eunice was frowning. 'What do you think the surprise is?' she asked me, as Eric parked the car. This took quite a long time. The space was narrow and he wasn't a very confident parker. We all had to get out and shout instructions at him.

'I don't know,' I said. 'It could be anything. He's mad, isn't he?'

Personally, I was hoping that the surprise was going to be a spending spree. Maybe he was so keen to impress Mam, he had decided to blow loads and loads of money on us. Maybe he would let us choose anything we wanted. Maybe he was trying to get into Mam's good books via crass material greed.

Great!

Ten minutes later, we were right inside the shopping mall. We were in one of the bits where four corridors met up in a central hub, with escalators and elevators and whatnot. Fountains were tinkling and muzak was playing. Hundreds of shoppers were strolling along, laden down with their purchases.

'What's this?' I said.

A large crowd was gathering. There were TV cameras. There was excitement in the air.

Mam was clutching Eric's arm. She gathered Eunice and me to her. 'Now, girls,' she said. 'Eric found out this was going to happen. He saw it on the local news at lunchtime. I'm sorry there wasn't time to warn you . . .'

'It's *Teen Sensation*, isn't it?' Eunice asked. 'It is,

isn't it? It's the public auditions for *Teen Sensation*! *KOF KOF KOF!*'

Eric was checking his watch worriedly.

Mam nodded at Eunice, biting her lip. 'They've been holding auditions all day. If I'd known, I'd have let you bunk school. But we booked you a place, as soon as we knew. And you're on – in about five minutes!'

'What?' Eunice looked dazed and appalled. 'I can't! I'm in my school clothes! *KOF!* I—!'

'You've got to!' Mam cried. 'You just have to! After me and Eric have gone to all this effort! You can't let us down now . . .'

'Erm,' I said. 'You haven't booked me in for an audition, have you? I'm not a teenager yet.'

'We tried,' Mam said sadly. 'But they wouldn't make any exceptions. I'm afraid only Eunice can get up there and do her stuff today.'

'No, Mam!' Eunice gibbered. 'I'm not ready! I can't! I need to mentally prepare myself . . .!'

'Rubbish!' Mam shouted. 'Now, you get yourself up there when they call your name, little lady. This is your big chance. And I'm not going to let you ruin it!'

This was brilliant! Suddenly, all the attention was off me, and I didn't have to worry about auditioning or any of that stuff. I could just stand back, with Mam and Eric, and enjoy the spectacle of Eunice getting herself in a nervous tizz and just about cacking herself.

We found ourselves some seats up near the front of the makeshift *Teen Sensation* stage. We watched a few losers come on and dance about and sing pretty terribly. And we booed them! It was great! Me, Mam and Eric had a great time in amongst the crowd, yelling 'Get off! You're rubbish! Booo!' And we got ready for Eunice's turn. She was going to sing some old Madonna number. She had disappeared behind the scenes to get herself ready.

'Won't it be great,' Mam said, 'if she gets herself onto *Teen Sensation?*'

I made up my mind to cheer her, whatever happened. She might be a lanky and awkward cow of a sister to me, but this was a talent show. This was *TV.* It was a serious business, and I had to give Eunice every ounce of support I could.

'HURRAY! HURRAY!' The three of us screamed ourselves hoarse when Eunice came on. Other members of the audience gave us funny looks for getting so carried away, but we didn't care. And Eunice looked brilliant! She'd backcombed her hair and switched her uniform about a bit so it was sexy. She looked a bit startled under the bright lights and with the cameras on her.

'Come on, Eunice!' Eric screamed, with that huge deep voice of his. It was just as loud as it had been at the car bootie. 'Give it your all! Make us proud, Eunice!'

The music started.

The deep throbbing bass. The cheesy synthesisers.

Eunice started bopping about. She flashed her legs around and hopped up and down.

We were all clapping along. The rest of the audience started clapping along too.

Eunice had us all in the palm of her hand!

Then she opened her mouth to start singing.

Bad move!

Chapter Seven

After that, Eric went quite serious and thoughtful. We had never seen him like that. We were used to happy-go-lucky Eric. Daft Eric. Messing-about Eric. But, after our Eunice got up on that stage in the shopping mall and shocked everyone with her warbling warthog act, Eric went very quiet.

Eunice got down off the stage and came to find us. The jeering and laughter were still ringing in her ears. Mam hugged her hard. I could see that Mam was alarmed, though. Eunice had never sung quite as badly as she had that night.

'Oh, my pet!' Mam cried, rubbing her back. 'Don't take any notice of them. What does this crowd know about singing? We thought you were marvellous!'

Eunice raised her teary, blotchy face and stared at Mam. '*KOF*. Do you really think so?'

'Err, um,' said Mam.

'Was I really marvellous?'

'Well,' said Mam. She was stalled. 'Let's get back to the car and get home, eh? We can order in pizzas, if you like.'

'I was awful, wasn't I?' Eunice wailed, her whole body starting to shake with sobs. 'That's why they were laughing at me! They thought I was terrible!'

I kept out of this.

Curiously, so did Eric. This was the point when he started looking thoughtful. 'Come on,' he said. 'Let's get back to the car.'

The idea of our shopping spree was forgotten. Mam and Eunice just wanted to get out of that place as soon as possible. I was really disappointed. All because our Eunice had made a drongo of herself in public! Why should I be punished for that? Still, I thought, as we hurried up the escalators and down the long marble halls to our exit, it was all worth it to see Eunice make a complete idiot of herself. How funny was that? Maybe now she'd have the sense to give up her stardom dreams for ever. Surely now she would see that she didn't stand a chance?

'Hey,' I said, as we left the mall and went searching for our car in the multi-storey. 'Do you think they'll show Eunice's audition turn on the telly?' They had a special section where they showed all the most abominable auditions. Eunice would surely be on that. I was only trying to cheer her up, but she started wailing again, and Mam turned to mouth some rude words at me.

Then we found the car and Eric drove us out of there, racketing and bouncing along the road, looking for a pizza joint on the way home.

'You're very quiet,' Mam accused him.

'Hmm,' he said thoughtfully.

'Are you okay?' Mam said. It was like she thought he might be in a bad mood.

'I'm just thinking,' he said, gritting his teeth and wrestling with the steering wheel as we went round a roundabout.

'What about?' Mam persisted.

'I think I'm about to have an idea.'

'An idea?'

Eric nodded grimly. 'A stupendous idea. A really and utterly fantastic idea. Just pipe down for a bit, will you?'

'Okay,' Mam shrugged, and stared out of the passenger window for the rest of the journey home. The sunset was all spectacular that evening: like orange and purple flames licking over the city's horizon. But Mam just looked peeved. I could tell. Her oldest daughter had proved to be a singing and dancing idiot. Eunice had turned out to be even less talented than any of us had suspected! And now Mam was thinking that her new bloke was in a big almighty huff.

But he wasn't. I knew that Eric was thinking things over, as he had promised. I knew it was true: he was on the verge of a really stupendous idea. We pulled into a retail park on the way home – one of those places with a giant carpet shop and a giant settee shop – because we knew there was a fantastic pizza takeaway there. I was despatched to go and fetch them. Mam and Eunice were too depressed to go, and Eric was thinking too hard. He gave me a twenty-pound note and I hopped out of the car, pleased with myself, because no one had ever trusted me with a twenty-pound note before.

Ten minutes later I came struggling out with boxes of pizza, cartons of fries, beakers of sticky sweet drinks, clunking with ice. Eric's face was all lit up.

'What is it?'

'I've had my idea!' He was grinning like a maniac. 'And I'm not telling anyone about it till we get home!'

We all sat together on our three-piece suite, with slices of hot pizza slowly dripping cheese in our hands. We were waiting on Eric, who was clearly relishing every moment.

'Well?' Mam burst out impatiently. 'What's this great idea of yours?'

'Wowwowowow!' he went. 'Hot pepperoni!' He swallowed, eyes watering.

'Get on with it, Eric!' Mam urged.

'Right,' he said. 'I think I know how Eunice and Helen can make it in showbiz.'

Eunice looked like she was going to cry again. She looked like she never wanted to sing ever again in her life.

'Oh yes?' said Mam, sceptically.

'Yes,' said Eric. 'I think I have thought up a way for Eunice and Helen to get through auditions. To get through all the rounds of auditions, of any TV talent show. I've discovered how they can get themselves into the quarter-finals, and the semi-finals and then the final itself! I think I know the way that they can make sure that they win!'

We were all on tenterhooks by now, as Eric cranked up the suspense. 'Howhowhow?' I shouted.

He grinned. 'You sing like an angel, Helen. You know that. We all know that. And Eunice sings like a horrible grunting warthog. That's what I found out tonight.'

Eunice's chin trembled. Her mouth dropped open, full of chewed pizza. 'Maaaaam!' she wailed. 'Your boyfriend is being horrible to me!'

'He's not my boyfriend,' Mam snapped. 'And what are you doing, Eric, being horrible to poor Eunice?'

He looked serious again. 'We have to face the truth. Eunice sings like a warbling warthog. She's appalling! She's atrocious! She was laughed off the stage tonight – and rightly so!'

'Maaaaam!' Eunice wailed.

I must admit, I wanted to laugh.

'Listen,' said Eric. 'The thing is, what I've decided you've got to do, is team up. Be a double act! Make up for each other's deficiencies.'

I didn't like the sound of this.

'Deficiencies?' said Mam.

'You've said before how weird it is that Helen doesn't get anywhere in auditions, even though she's got the voice of an angel. Well, we all know why that is, don't we?'

'Because she's a stroppy little madam?' Mam asked, eyeing me.

But I knew what Eric was going to say.

'No! Because she's little and not very pretty and her hair's a terrible mess! She always looks awful!'

Mam looked shocked. 'Eric!' she screamed. Eunice looked smug.

'It's all right, Mam,' I said. 'I don't mind. He's only telling the truth.'

'They'll never pick her, because she doesn't look right,' Eric said, ploughing on bravely. 'But Eunice, on the other hand, looks exactly right, with her long blonde hair and her clear skin and her long legs and everything.'

'A double act?' Eunice said, looking sickly.

'That's right. And Helen could drown your voice out, so no one would have to hear you at all. Maybe you could even just open and close your mouth and let her do all the singing instead.'

Mam was biting her lip. 'It might work, I suppose . . .'

Eunice was looking at me haughtily. She looked like being on a stage with me was the worst thing she could imagine.

'I'm surprised you've never thought of it before,' Eric said, gobbling up his pepperoni and looking very pleased with himself.

'Thing is,' Mam said. 'Lots of these shows aren't for groups or double acts. They're for individuals. The next one coming up, *Diva Wars*: that's just for individuals. They won't let double acts on there.'

'Hmm,' said Eric. 'You're right there, Marjorie.'

Eunice and I exchanged a look. It was a long time since we'd heard anyone call Mam Marjorie. It was like we had just about forgotten her proper name!

'And *Diva Wars* is the best show, isn't it?' Eric

said. 'That's the one that either of you girls would dearly love to win?'

Eunice nodded firmly. And even I had to agree. *Diva Wars* was fantastic. The winner got a recording deal on the spot, all the best designers and hair stylists at their beck and call, and a world tour all worked out for them. A *world* tour! Even I would be made up to win *Diva Wars*. It was brilliant! I'd get to see the whole world!

'Then I need to do some more thinking,' Eric said, starting to shovel fry after fry after fry in his gob. 'There will be a way round this. You'll see. You leave it with Eric. I'll find a way. I have the most wonderful ideas. Every time! You'll see!'

All three of us watched him cramming his gullet with chips. By then we really believed him. Of course Eric would find a way!

His eyes lit up.

He said, 'Remember Loulabelle Radcliffe, who won *Search for a Celeb* two years ago?'

We thought back. 'Was she the one with one eye?' Mam suddenly said.

'That's right!' Eric beamed. 'One huge big eye, smack in the middle of her forehead! Like a Martian, or something! And wasn't it a heart-warming spectacle? The girl with only one eye and her lovely, inspirational show tunes?'

We all looked at each other. What was Eric's big idea going to be?

'And what about Belladonna Arkwright, eh? Last year's winner on *Star Turn?*'

We all knew the answer to that. 'No eyebrows!' we chorused.

'And Tony Tomorrow? The wonder boy of *Talent Parade?*'

'A huge head and no nose!' we all shouted back.

'Do you see a theme developing here?' Eric grinned.

We frowned. We weren't sure.

'Is it . . . overcoming adversity?' Eunice said. 'Still managing to be a star, even when the odds are stacked against you?' She sounded very emotional as she said this.

'Well, kind of,' Eric said. 'But I was thinking, more like – you have to have something *wrong* with you!'

'WHAT?'

'It's true! The audience at home has to feel sorry for you! "Ah, look at her! She's tone deaf and she's got ears like a great big elephant! Let's phone in and vote for her!" "Oh, that poor boy. He looks like a dolphin. Let's text our vote in for him!" Don't you see? Sympathy is the new big thing! You have to stir

75

their heartstrings! That's how you really shine, girls! That's how you really get to succeed!'

'Well, our Helen's a dwarf,' Mam said. 'How come she hasn't succeeded, then?'

'Ah,' said Eric. 'That's easy. It's not exotic enough. Being a dwarf isn't exciting, like having a freakish, Martian-style eye in the middle of your forehead. It's not like having tentacles for arms, or no nose or eyebrows! It's just normal! It's just being small!'

Eric grinned at me and I grinned back at him through a mouthful of pizza.

'So?' Mam said. 'What are you suggesting?'

Eric cleared his throat grandly. 'I don't know how you'll feel about this. You see, in a way it's cheating. In a way it'll be dishonest. I'm not sure you'll go along with it. I'm not sure at all . . .'

'Just tell us!' Mam screeched.

'Yes! We need to know!' Eunice shouted. Funny how her dreams of stardom were flooding back to her, even after the evening's humiliation. 'Tell us how we can win *Diva Wars!*'

'Okay,' said Eric. 'Here's my plan. We play to both your strengths, right? Helen's magnificent voice, and Eunice's looks. We compensate for Helen's looks and Eunice's warbling warthog voice. Now, how do we do this?'

'HOW??' yelled Mam and Eunice in unison.

I think I could already see what was coming.

'With a great big shoe,' Eric said.

'WHAT??'

He laughed at our confusion. He really loved being the centre of attention. 'Have you ever heard of Siamese twins? Of conjoined twins?'

We looked at each other.

'Well, yes,' I said. 'That's when twins have been joined together since birth. Their bodies are attached, at the head or the waist sometimes. And they have to go around with each other all their lives! And sometimes they go in for a really dangerous operation to try to get separated ...' I'd read about them and seen a few things on the TV. They were really amazing stories. Brave and sometimes tragic stories. I had wondered what it must be like, to go around with your sister like that: the two of you belonging to one body. It was really hard to imagine.

Mam looked shocked. 'Oh, Eric, you can't be suggesting ...'

Eunice was lost. 'What? What is he suggesting? Tell me!' Eunice can be a bit dim sometimes.

Eric told us: 'I think you should pretend to be Siamese twins. You have been joined together, at the foot, since birth. And that's how you audition

77

for *Diva Wars*. As a double act – but in one single body!'

There was a very dramatic pause after he came out with his idea.

Then it was me who broke the silence.

'Joined together . . . at the *foot*?!'

Chapter Eight

Meanwhile, Mam and Eric were starting to go out with each other.

'What, do you really think so?' Eunice hissed. We were in our bedroom, talking this over.

'Yes, I reckon they are,' I hissed back. 'I think they're *seeing each other*.'

We both knew this was a ridiculous phrase for it. It was a grown-up kind of phrase.

'Seeing each other!' Eunice said, looking disgusted. 'Hmm.' She looked like she was thinking up schemes for getting rid of him. A few of her schemes had worked really well in the past. Like when she had sent Dirty Barry packing. He was Mam's last-but-one boyfriend. He was a biker, and we didn't like Mam tearing about the town on the back of his bike. Eunice had also managed to get rid of Neville, who worked at the town hall. Even Mam herself hadn't been that keen on Neville.

'I can't believe she'd let herself be seen in public

with Eric,' Eunice sighed. She flopped down on her pink and fluffy bed. 'He's such a state! He's so common!'

I didn't like her slagging him off.

'What do you think of this plan of his?' Eunice said. 'It's mad, isn't it? We'd never get away with it.'

I shrugged. 'He's right, though. We'll never get anywhere on our own. Not with your warthog voice.'

She frowned. 'Or your ugly pixie looks.'

'Huh,' I said.

'We could give it a go, I suppose,' Eunice sighed. 'If being a star really means so much to you . . .'

I opened my mouth to protest.

'I mean,' added Eunice. 'What can they do to us if we got found out? *KOF KOF KOF*. It's not something you can be put in prison for, is it – pretending to be Siamese twins?'

'I don't suppose so,' I said.

'And what if we won, eh?' Eunice's eyes were gleaming. She was staring up at our bedroom ceiling. In the cracked plaster she could see her whole showbiz future mapped out. The costumes and concerts; the records and the fans queuing up and screaming at us. 'We would be massive!' she said. 'Everyone would be so nice to us! Just because we were joined together at the foot! Eric's right!

They wouldn't dare not let us win! All artistic judgement would fly out of the window!'

'Hurray!' I said, feebly. Then I looked at her lying there: all skinny and smug, dreaming up our twinned future. 'But could we stand it, though? Being forced to stay together all that time? Being tied together like the three-legged race?'

Eunice shrugged. 'Who cares? If we're famous, who cares? I'd put up with anything for that.'

She meant it! She really meant it!

'And anyway,' Eunice went on. 'We're forced to be together all the time, aren't we? In the same school, the same family, even the same bedroom! And we've absolutely nothing in common, have we?' She looked me up and down, disgustedly.

'No,' I said. 'I don't reckon we have.'

'So . . . we might as well go along with Eric's crazy scheme,' she said. 'We really haven't got anything to lose, have we?'

I still wasn't sure, though. It really felt like we were considering doing something very wrong. What about all the real, genuine conjoined twins out there? Would they be mad at us? Would they think we were making fun of them and their joined-together plight?

I got into my pyjamas, mulling this over. Or maybe . . . the conjoined twins of the world would see us as real heroes. We'd be the most famous Siamese twins on the planet!

I couldn't be sure. It still seemed wrong to me. And I hated the idea of being tied to Eunice all the time. The very thought gave me the shivers.

That night I dreamed about a wedding in the moonlight. There was confetti everywhere and champagne corks popping. I often dreamed about weddings, but this was different. This was the wedding of Mam and Eric. They were standing at the altar with tears in their eyes. They were so happy to be there. They both looked gorgeous. And the church was heaving with well-wishers. There were more people there than we even know. But where were Eunice and I? Why weren't we up at the front, dressed in bridesmaids' gowns?

Then I realised we *were* there, in the aisle. We were tied together. We were dressed as a yellow and pink-spotted pantomime horse, and we were galloping up and down, whinnying and neighing like mad. I was the bum. The bum! And Eunice was the horse's head: fluttering its ridiculous eyelashes and trying to get all the attention.

After school the next day, Eric had another trip out in the car planned.

'Oh god, do we have to?' Eunice squirmed. 'I hate

his car. It's so tiny. I have to sit all cramped up in the back.'

'I don't mind it,' I said. I knew Eunice was thinking about the helicopter Mam had been promising her for as long as we could remember. That was the real mark of stardom for my mam: not having to bother with roads or cars at all – or even the ground! Real stars just swooped about wherever they wanted to go, in helicopters.

Eunice was really twisting her face. 'Where are we going?'

'A little surprise,' Eric said. Immediately we started thinking it might be a shopping trip. If we were going to be conjoined, we'd probably need a whole new, matching wardrobe, wouldn't we? And we'd need that giant shoe, like he said, for our shared foot . . .

'You haven't seen where I live,' he said. 'I thought we might go there for tea tonight.'

Mam turned round in her seat as Eric started the engine. She gave us a sickly smile. It was like: don't you let me down, girls. Don't start playing up. Be nice to Eric.

Eunice just went, 'Huh!' and sat back with her arms folded. I didn't mind. I was interested to see where Eric lived – with his mam.

It was no secret that Eric still lived at home with

his mam. 'She dotes on me, the poor old thing,' he had said. 'I couldn't have left her to manage on her own.'

Anyway, now this poor old dear – as he kept calling her – was keen on meeting all of us. She was making tea for us.

'She wants to meet my new girlfriend,' Eric said, in a soppy voice, as he trundled us along in his car.

'Girlfriend!' Eunice spat, and made throwing up noises.

'Eunice!' warned Mam.

'Is it true, then?' Eunice said. 'Are you two *seeing* each other?'

Mam told us that that was indeed true. Eunice shuddered. 'Oh, god,' she said again, glaring at the hairy back of Eric's neck and his baseball cap facing the wrong way. Her face said it all: now we're *stuck* with him!

We drove further out of town than I was expecting. Suddenly there were patches of green and hills and loads of trees. We went right out of the city and into the countryside. 'Do you live somewhere posh, Eric?' I piped up from the back. He and Mam just laughed at this.

'Not really, love,' he said. 'It's a little, old village. Mam's lived there all her life nearly.'

The village was called Broad Bottom, and was at the bottom of a very leafy valley, in the deep shadow of a viaduct.

'Oh, it looks gorgeous,' Mam said, peering out at the old stone buildings and their well-tended gardens.

'It's early summer,' said Eric. 'You're seeing it at its best. Come the winter we get snowed in and all sorts.'

'I wouldn't mind!' said Mam. 'It looks like heaven to me. Eh, girls? After some of the estates we've lived on.'

We pulled up outside a black-and-white pub with a slate roof. It was called The Dirty Duck. I thought Mam and Eric were maybe going in for a drink to make themselves brave before meeting his mam. But this, it turned out, was where he lived! His mother *owned* The Dirty Duck. She was standing in the cosy saloon bar as we arrived.

And guess what?

She was a dwarf!

She had dark purple hair and she wore just as much clunky gold jewellery as Eric. She was all dressed up in a black off-the-shoulder jumper and a tight skirt. At her age! But she looked really glam, that was the thing. She was all dolled up in make-up and I realised that's what she looked like: a little doll of a glamorous older lady.

She grabbed hold of me and Eunice and hugged us with all her might. 'Oh, it's the girls!' she cackled. Her voice was raucous with cigarettes. 'Oh, and Eric's told me so much about you two! How you're both so gorgeous and talented. Let me look at you!' She surveyed us up and down, nodding. 'Lovely girls! Eunice, you're the tall one, aren't you? And so you must be Helen, eh?' She grinned at me. Her sparkly earrings were so heavy they were swinging about.

But the most amazing thing about Eric's mam, Marlene, was that she was even smaller than I was! I just about fell over with shock. She was about the size of a toddler. Well, maybe not *that* small, but nearly. She had to reach up to pat me on the head.

She turned to Mam. 'And you're Marjorie, are you?' she said, narrowing her eyes and having a good look at our mam. 'You're the one who's stolen my poor boy's heart, eh?'

Mam looked embarrassed and flattered and girlish, all at once. She looked pleased, too. The old-fashioned bar around us was pretty full of old fellas from the village. They were watching with interest as the tiny Marlene fussed over us and said we were the most glamorous new arrivals they'd had in years at The Dirty Duck.

Eunice caught my eye, in the middle of all this commotion and mouthed the word: 'Midget!' Then she bent to whisper in my ear: 'What is this? KOF. A whole family of freaks?'

'You're a freak too, Eunice,' I whispered back. 'You're as big a freak as the rest of us!'

She looked like she wanted to punch me for this. 'I am not! No way! I'm perfect!'

'Hah!' I said. 'But you're going to be a freak, aren't you? You're going to turn yourself into one! Me and you – we're going to be freaks together!'

Marlene was lifting up the bar and showing us through to the back. 'Yoo hoo! Come on, girls! Come through to my special parlour and have some tea. I've got cakes and chocolate biscuits and everything. And the two of you can tell me all about your plans for stardom!'

Eunice and I winced. We glared at Eric. What had he told this tiny purple-haired woman about us?

We followed them into the parlour, where a lavish tea was all nicely laid out on a low table. It was just the right height for me! Amazing! And all the prettily-patterned china cups and plates were exactly the right size for me and Marlene. Mam, Eric and Eunice had to crouch down on cushions, close to the floor, but me and Marlene were happily perched on doll-sized chairs.

'What a lovely spread!' Mam cried, as Marlene urged us to eat.

The woman had gone mad with preparations! She had made sherry trifle, and green jelly, and Victoria sponge, and flans and pavlova and fairy cakes. She had even done those space-age-type grapefruit with the cocktail sticks stuck in and bits of pineapple, cheese and sausage.

'Eat up, everyone! There's no point being shy!'

Everyone started digging in. Eric was looking so pleased and proud that we were all together. He watched over us, and for a while he seemed worried at how quiet the three of us were. But then he saw that we were just shy with his mam. He really wanted us all to get on, you could tell. In a flash, I saw that he was beaming with happiness – he was almost too happy to eat – because his favourite people were all in this room together. My heart went out to Eric just then. More than it ever had.

As we ate, I realised that the walls were filled with framed black-and-white photos and posters. In them, a much younger Marlene was standing with various showbiz types: singers and magicians; footballers and film stars. And the posters were lists of people appearing on the bill of old-fashioned theatres. Her name was up there again and again:

Marlene Higginbottom. In the photos she looked glamorous, sexy and very very small.

And I realised, all of a sudden. In her own time and, in her own way, Marlene had been a star!

But you could tell. You could tell just by looking at her. Even now, all these years later, Eric's tiny mother was every inch a star.

Chapter Nine

It was a brilliant night at The Dirty Duck. I was thinking it all over as Eric drove us back into the city. Eunice and I were dozing in the back of his car, and Mam and Eric were talking quietly up front. Outside, the countryside was dark and looming. Gradually it disappeared, to be replaced by the more familiar orange-and-pink glow of the city lights.

For most of the journey home there was a great feeling of contentment in Eric's knackered old car. We had eaten everything at Marlene's buffet. 'You would think they were never fed,' Mam had said, embarrassed by us. But even Mam had loosened up and enjoyed herself. Eunice, too, had found less to complain about than usual.

In the saloon bar, Eric had fixed up a grand-looking karaoke machine. It had, he claimed, over seven thousand songs on it! Surely we would all find something to sing on it. So, for the benefit of the old regulars from Broad Bottom, me and Eunice got up and gave them a few songs. Or rather, we both got up, and I did the singing. We were halfway into our first number when I realised what was happening. I looked up at Eunice and realised that she was just opening and closing her mouth. She was dancing away and doing all the moves – but she was miming! I had to sing louder, then. I had to sing for both of us.

The old men and women drinking at The Dirty Duck gave us a huge round of applause.

Marlene was grinning enthusiastically. She took my face in her hands. 'You've got it! The fairies must have sprinkled that certain something in your cot when you were a baby!'

'Yeah,' scoffed Eunice. 'Rat poison!'

Marlene just laughed at this, assuming that Eunice wasn't meaning to be nasty.

Then Marlene herself got up and did a song for the bar. Eric operated the gleaming karaoke machine, smiling with pride. He leaned over and whispered to me that this song was one of his mother's favourites. It was her show-stopper, back when she was touring all the pubs and clubs when she was young in the Seventies.

Show-stopper was the right word. Marlene had a huge voice. It was hard to see how it was all coming out of that tiny woman. It was like a vast and powerful genie coming out of a little lamp. She flung back her head and roared out this dramatic love ballad, and had us all hooked and just about weeping. We applauded wildly when she was done.

'It isn't often Mam does that,' Eric said, over the noise of the cheers, 'and goes back to her past. She wanted to do it for you lot, I think. To show you how she used to sing.'

I decided that Marlene was the best thing ever. I gave her a huge hug out in the car park, where she came to wave us off. I felt like I had known her all my life.

'We have to get these two back,' Mam was saying. 'It's a school night, and I don't know what their teachers would say if they knew they'd been in the pub all night!'

'Ha!' Marlene laughed. 'They'll learn more performing songs like that than they would at their school, I bet.'

She said such cool things! I hugged her again. And here's the amazing thing – so did Eunice! Eunice, who never shows anyone any affection. Who's above all that kind of thing and just gets sarcastic.

'You're a good girl,' Marlene told her. 'You make sure you look after your mam and your sister.

They're precious.' For a moment I thought I saw Eunice's eyes flash. I knew she was thinking: but *I'm* the precious one! I'm the *most* precious!

'You've got two marvellous girls there,' Marlene told Mam, reaching up to kiss her cheek.

'I know that,' Mam said stiffly.

'I'm really glad you're all going to be a part of our family,' Eric's mam smiled.

Then we were off. We piled into Eric's car and we went zooming back into the city.

We were quiet – contentedly quiet – for most of the journey back. Eric didn't even put one of his CDs on, which was unusual for him. I think we all still had the cheerful and spangling echoes of the karaoke in our heads. Eunice's lanky body slumped sideways and she dozed, leaning against me.

It was as we went past the multiplex cinema and the all-night supermarket, and we were well and truly back on our own territory, that Mam started kicking off. I knew it was going to happen. I could tell by the angle of her head, by the way she was sitting in the passenger seat. By the atmosphere she was suddenly giving off. I knew her too well. And I knew that anything good, like that night had been, can't be left for long like that. It has to be spoiled. I don't know what it is about Mam that makes her do this. It's just what she always does.

Next to her, Eric still looked happy and pleased that the night of introductions had gone so well.

We were about five minutes from home and Mam started muttering: '"You've got two marvellous girls there." Ha! As if I didn't know! Like I need to be told how many daughters I've got and what they're like!'

'What was that, love?' asked Eric, concentrating on the road.

'Well, who does she think she is?' Mam said, more loudly now, as she started to lose her temper. 'And what did she mean by that: "I'm glad you're going to be part of our family"? *Our* family? *Hers*? That's so big-headed! That's so self-centred! What is she? The centre of the universe? There's more of us than there are you and her. Why isn't it that *I'm* letting you two join *our* family, eh? Isn't that more like it? Why does she have to be in the middle of it all?'

Eric looked at her, worried. 'I don't know what you mean. Why are you shouting? I thought we had a nice time . . .'

Eunice raised her head off my shoulder and sat up in alarm.

'Nice time!' Mam said. 'Nice time? It was terrible! She was so patronising and nasty. She just wants to own everyone and take them over. And then we have to stand and watch her get up and sing! It was awful! Some horrible old song in front of a pub of boozed-up old people!'

Eric looked at her and, even in the dim light, I could see he was hurt by her words. 'But you seemed to be having a nice time tonight. A few gin-and-oranges and you didn't feel so shy any more. I thought you liked meeting my mam, and the two of you seemed to get on so well ...' His voice shook slightly.

'I was pretending!' Mam cried. 'Do you really think I enjoyed any of that? Being dragged out of my home to sit in some dingy pub and watch an old woman show off? And just about steal my kids off me?'

'What?!'

'I was pretending for your sake, you silly fat oaf. I thought that you would want me and your mother to get along. Because you're so attached to her, apparently.'

Eric fell quiet. He turned to face the empty road ahead. He applied himself to his driving. We were almost home.

'I don't think we'll be wanting to go out there again, thanks, Eric,' Mam said. 'To that pub. What was it called? The Dirty Duck?' She laughed bitterly. 'And I don't really think my girls should be going to pubs on school nights, do you?'

'Maybe not,' he said gruffly. 'I just wanted you all to meet. I thought it would be nice.'

'I think we've had enough of your ideas for a while.' Mam's voice had gone hard. I knew this was the most dangerous sign. It was how her voice went just before a strop. A mega-strop. 'It was your rubbishy idea to make Eunice get up in that shopping mall and sing. You forced her to make an idiot of herself in front of the cameras!'

'I thought it was what she wanted to do! You said so yourself, Marjorie!'

'Shut up,' she snapped. 'I can't bear weak, blubbering men.'

'Mam,' I spoke up, as the car veered round into the entrance of our estate. 'We had a really lovely time at Eric's mam's house. I think you're spoiling it.'

There. I'd said it. It had taken me all of my courage to lean forward and say this. But I had to. I couldn't let Eric think that Mam was speaking the truth. She was just in one of her self-destructive moods. Nothing was safe from her tongue. No one was.

She was quiet for a few moments.

Then: 'Sit back in your seat. You shouldn't lean

96

forward like that when he's driving. It's dangerous. He's not a very confident driver as it is. Do you want to get killed, Helen? Do you want to go flying through the windscreen?'

I sat back. Wow. Mam was in a *really* bad mood tonight.

Eunice leaned across in the dark and patted my hand. Really, she did! She had never done that before.

Then we pulled up in front of our house. Mam flung the car door open and jumped out, front-door keys ready in her hand. Eric watched her, frowning in dismay. 'Is she often like this, girls?'

'Yeah,' I said. 'This is pretty much a regular thing.'

'No it's not!' Eunice protested. 'Just sometimes, it all gets a bit much for her.'

Mam was struggling with the front-door lock. We heard her swear loudly.

'I thought tonight was a big success,' Eric said sadly.

'It was! It really was!' I burst out, and kissed him on the cheek.

Even Eunice said, 'Thank you, Eric. It was a very nice trip out.'

Then we got out of the car. Mam had managed to get into the house. All the lights in the kitchen, the hallway, and the upstairs went on, suddenly and blindingly. Our house was like a spaceship about to take off.

'She won't want me to come in,' Eric said, sadly.

Mam appeared on the doorstep, hands on hips. 'Are you two coming in? Or are you going to sit out in the street all night? It's very late! School tomorrow!'

'We have to go in,' I told Eric.

'I'm off, Marjorie,' he said, his voice all hopeful and too loud in the night-time street.

'Yeah?' she said. 'Okay, then. Don't let us keep you.'

Eric looked down and said to me, 'Look after her, will you? I'll phone tomorrow.'

Mam went manic round about midnight. On went the washing machine and the dryer in the kitchen. She put the radio on so loud she had next door knocking on the paper-thin walls. She went round with the hoover, too. She was crowding out our whole place with noise.

'Milkshakes!' she yelled out, pulling her blender out of the cupboard and trying to remember how to fit it together. 'Them bananas have gone black. Let's make milkshakes!'

'Mam,' Eunice said. 'It's after midnight. We need to sleep. It's too late for milkshakes now.'

Eunice and I were standing there in our pyjamas, trying to say the right thing. The thing that would get her to calm down and go to bed.

'Oh,' she said. 'You won't have a milkshake, will you not? But you'll have her jelly and trifle and perfect sponge cake, won't you? You'll take them off a perfect stranger and you'll be all polite. You were both so polite and well-behaved all night!'

'That's *good*, isn't it?' I said.

'No!' Mam yelled. 'It's not what you're like for me! *I'm* the one who has to have you twenty-four seven! *I'm* the one who sees what horrible, spoiled, wicked brats you really are! No one else has to stop you squabbling and fighting all the time! No one else has to do everything for you, because you're both so lazy! And then you go giving complete strangers like that old cow the impression that you're perfect! That you're *marvellous daughters*! And you're not! You're horrible! You've both ruined my life!'

Eunice burst into tears at this, of course.

Mam didn't give up. She was mashing the black bananas into the blender, and getting ready to give it an almighty whizz. 'I feel like . . . I feel like you preferred that old dwarfy woman to me! And you prefer fat bloody Eric to me! Who are they to you? You've only known them five minutes! They haven't known you all your lives like I have! I'm everything to you girls, and don't you forget it!'

We nodded. 'Yes, Mam.'

Then she switched on the blender with a huge swooshing noise.

Chapter Ten

'I'm sure if you ring him, it'll be fine,' I said.

I was bunking off school. Eunice had already gone. Good girl, Eunice. She wouldn't ever get into trouble. At ten o'clock in the morning, I was giving my mam black coffee and a plate of burned, dry toast. She was sitting at our kitchen bench in her dressing gown with her hair looking awful. In fact, all of her looked awful.

'I don't think Eric will mind,' I said. 'He's not like that. He'll understand. He cares about you.'

Mam put her head in her hands. I couldn't make out what she was saying.

This would last for most of the morning. We had been through this scene quite a few times before. This morning, unfortunately, there was no car bootie for us to catch a taxi to. There was nothing to distract Mam from the misery of her hangover and herself.

'What it is, you see, Helen, is that I'm like a lioness with her cubs.'

I sat down opposite her. I'd had the lioness-with-her-cubs speech before, too.

'And I get very protective over you and Eunice. You know I do. So when other people come too close, like Eric and his mother . . . well, then I tend to snap and lash out.' She looked at me, very white-faced. 'Do you think I've messed it all up? And scared him off? Do you think he'll have anything more to do with me?'

I'd made myself some black coffee too. Usually I wasn't allowed to have too much black, treacly, espresso because – get this – Mam worried it would stunt my growth! Even more! But I figured I could get away with having what I wanted this morning, what with Mam feeling so guilty.

'I think he was really upset last night,' I said. 'He's never seen you like that.'

'I'm volatile! I'm sensitive! I feel things very deeply!'

'Hmm,' I said, sipping my coffee and swinging my legs on the stool.

'I really don't want to spoil things with Eric,' Mam said thoughtfully. 'Who'd have thought it? I must be, like . . . falling for him or something. A big oaf like that!'

102

'You should stop calling him that,' I said.

'He doesn't care.'

'I don't think he liked you calling his mam names,' I said. 'I think he minded a lot about that.'

Mam cringed. 'Oh, I didn't, did I?'

'You said some awful things about her. And you said she was trying to take your daughters off you.'

Mam cursed herself. 'I'm such an idiot.'

'I thought Marlene was great,' I said.

'Huh,' said Mam. 'You would.'

'What, because she's more on my level?' I caught Mam's eye and we both had a laugh about that.

'I'll give him a ring and grovel for a while,' Mam sighed. She got up to examine the washing machine which, in her fury last night, she had stuffed too full. 'He'll forgive me. He can't believe his luck, going out with me in the first place,' she said. 'I'm way out of his league.'

'Mam . . .!' I warned.

'I know, I know, I'm an awful person.' She yanked open the washer door. 'Look at this! Everything's all mixed together and everything's run!'

Sure enough, we were having fish-finger sandwiches at teatime when there was a knock at the back door. Mam went to answer it, and there was Eric, hiding his face behind a big bunch of roses. Even though

Mam's never been keen on roses – she thinks them old-fashioned – she hugged him and forgave him on the spot.

'I must have been winding you up something chronic,' Eric said, shambling down our hall like a big old Labrador, delighted to be let indoors. 'I must really have annoyed you, to make you shout and go on like that.'

'Well . . .' Mam said.

'Because you've got the sweetest nature in the world, haven't you?' said Eric.

Mam narrowed her eyes at him. 'Are you taking the mick?'

He grabbed her up, slobbering over her. 'Give us a kiss!' And then she was squealing and pretending to batter him with the roses.

Usually, with any of Mam's previous blokes I'd have felt sick at this display. Some bloke grabbing at her and kissing her in the front room. But with Eric, I didn't mind. With Eric there it seemed right. Eunice was sitting beside me and she looked politely away as Mam and Eric made their peace. Eunice was trying to eat her fish-finger sandwich daintily, with a napkin and everything. I was pleased to see a blob of ketchup on the front of her school blouse.

'Well, girls,' Eric said, making himself comfy, as

Mam went to whizz him a sandwich under the grill. 'You were both terrific last night. You certainly wowed my mam. And she knows what she's on about. She won *Starry Eyes* in 1974, only she's too modest to go on about it. But she knows all about these talent shows and, if you can impress *her*, you're really in with a chance.'

'Really!' I said. 'Did she *really* think we were good?'

'Huh,' said Eunice. 'What about me? Was I good, too?'

'You looked the part,' Eric said tactfully. 'You looked exactly like a popstar.'

Mam came back with a sandwich for Eric, which he took gratefully.

'I have this awful temper,' she said. 'I'm really sorry.'

He nodded.

Then the advert for *Diva Wars* came on.

Eunice grabbed the remote control and turned the sound up full blast.

She screeched over the noise. 'Auditions! Next week! Next week, here! That's sooner than we thought!'

As the noisy, almost unbearably exciting, advert finished, she sagged back down on the settee, her fish-fingers forgotten; dignity forgotten. Eunice looked extremely stressed. 'Next week!' she gasped. 'Next Saturday!'

Suddenly Eric was like a great general in the war. He went very serious and solemn. 'Then we have to get going, don't we? We have to put this plan into operation.'

'You mean Operation: Siam?' Mam said.

Eric nodded. He looked at us. 'That's if we are all agreed. This is a big thing, girls. It's a big opportunity, but it's also a big deception that we are intending to go ahead with.'

'Oh, we don't care,' said Mam. 'Let's do it! I don't have any scruples any more! Let's win, for once!'

'Girls?' Eric said. 'It will mean pretending to be twins, you know. Pretending that you've always been joined together. A lot of well-meaning people will believe in you. Can you go ahead with something like that?'

Eunice was frowning. She had seen a hole in the plan. 'What about school? *KOF. KOF. KOF.* We've been at this one for three months. People know us. They know we aren't the same age. They know we aren't joined together at the foot. What if we get on the show and someone phones in? *KOF.* And tells everyone that we're a fraud?'

Eric chomped his sandwich thoughtfully. 'Ah

yes. That is a problem, Eunice. You're right.'

'It's hopeless!' Mam cried out. 'Someone is bound to recognise them! We're bound to get rumbled by someone!'

'We'll change their names,' Eric shrugged. 'We'll say they're ... I don't know – Mary and Sue, or something.'

'I want to be Sue,' Eunice said. I shrugged.

'And if anyone says anything to you in the street or at school about the girls who are winning every round in *Diva Wars*, you can just shrug and say: "Yes, there is a passing resemblance to us, isn't there? But they aren't us. Obviously. We aren't joined together, are we?"'

'It sounds a bit dodgy,' Mam said thoughtfully.

'Of course it's dodgy!' Eric said. 'It's a great big whopping lie! That's why! But we have to stick together, and stick to our story. If we keep our cool we can get away with it. Seriously! Just think about winning! The recording contract! The designer-type clothes! The world tour! Just think about that!'

'I am,' said Mam. 'I am thinking about that.'

'You know,' said Eric, '*You* could have been a star, Marjorie. You should have been. You're gorgeous. My mam reckons that you could have been a movie star, with your looks.'

'Really?' Mam's eyes went wide. She hadn't had

a compliment like that in years. This one would keep her quiet for some time to come. Personally, I thought Eric was pushing it, slightly, with the flattery. Mam's pretty, of course she is – and of course I think she's the prettiest mam in the world. But I still think Eric was overdoing it, in the attempt to get back in her good books. Well – it didn't matter, so long as he stayed there, and we were all together.

Funny. We hadn't known him for that long but already he seemed such a major part of our lives. Him and his knackered car and his baseball hat and all his bling. Him and his mam and The Dirty Duck, which we went back to, for tea again, the following week – and our mam behaved herself afterwards this time. Him and his car booties and his stall of every kind of music in the world. We would join him there on each Sunday following that first time, and he would always get me to stand up and belt out a few favourites. It was my chance to star alone, in my own limelight, and I had to relish it. Once me and Eunice embarked on our double act, I would never be able to perform alone again.

That's just how it was going to be. Once you start on a lie, you have to stick to it.

When we were home and just ourselves, just two ordinary schoolgirls, we were Helen and Eunice.

But when we sang, when we were in the limelight, then we were Mary-Sue, in one single body, joined at the foot. And together – we were dynamite.

One day after school, Eric came round with a pile of shoe boxes.

We sat in the living room, full of anticipation.

'You have to get used to moving around together and being joined together,' Eric said. 'There's a real knack to it. Just like the three-legged race at sports day, remember? How you have to get into a rhythm of moving around with your middle legs tied together? And once you both know what you are doing, then you can even run.'

We nodded. 'Get on with it,' Eunice urged.

'This is important,' Eric said. 'You have to practise really hard together. Because it isn't just walking or running you'll have to do. You'll have to dance around the stage, too! All the special chore- ography that they expect on these talent shows, you'll have to be able to do that, as well. And you have to be better than everyone else!'

'Okay, okay,' we said. 'We'll practise! We'll practise day and night!'

It was already less than a week until the auditions for *Diva Wars*. Even though they were being held at the same hotel venue as our resounding failure in

Star Turn, we were both feeling pretty confident. Amazingly confident, actually. Even Eunice! It was as if we had pooled all our strength and talent and nerve. We felt like nothing could stand in our way!

This conjoined duo was going to knock everyone's socks off!

Then, almost ceremonially, Eric opened the three shoe boxes he had brought with him.

Inside lay three beautiful shoes. They were bright red and glittering, with heels and buckles and everything. They were extraordinary. Like something out of a fairy tale.

Mam gasped at them. 'Where did you get them . . .?'

'Believe it or not,' Eric said, 'but they are hand-stitched. Hand-made. Mam's got an old friend who's a shoemaker in the village. I explained our precise requirements to him.'

And here they were, nestled in cerise tissue paper. Eric picked them out and offered them to us.

'A left shoe for Eunice, in her exact size,' he said. 'A right shoe for Helen, in her exact size.' And then he held out the third shoe. 'And one for Eunice's right, and Helen's left, to share. A shoe big enough for the two of them.'

He looked like Prince Charming, kneeling there. Remember? When Prince Charming went calling round everyone's houses, in the days after the palace ball?

Except, in our case, the grand, fantastic, glittering ball hadn't happened yet. That was still to come!

And what's more, as we put on our new, hand-made shoes, Eunice and I certainly didn't feel like ugly sisters. We felt like beautiful, exotic, Siamese sisters!

Sisters who were destined to wipe the floor with all other contenders during *Diva Wars*!

Chapter Eleven

We did it, of course. It all worked out as Eric had planned. It was almost magical, the way things suddenly started to go right.

'I'm gobsmacked,' Mam kept saying, afterwards. 'You could knock me down with a feather.' At first she went white in the face and all the jubilation was sealed tight inside her, like she had turned into Tupperware. 'All that time trying,' she said. 'All the set-backs. And now ... Now we've made it, Eric!'

Eric was glowing with pleasure. 'Ah, now don't go celebrating yet. The girls are only just through to the next round of auditions ...'

'Yes, but – they've never made it this far before! This is a humungous triumph, Eric! And it's all down to you!'

'Huh,' whispered Eunice, glancing round at me. We were sitting side by side in the back of the taxi. Mam and Eric had splashed out, so we could return home in style. 'All down to him, she says!' Eunice sounded proper huffy. Her face was more like a smacked bum than ever. 'It was us who got through the audition!' she hissed. 'It was our talent and our star quality!'

I smiled quietly to myself. Yes, in one way, Eunice was right. When it came down to it, it had indeed been just the two of us, standing there in the audition room, under the full glare of the TV lights – getting scrutinised by the judging panel.

The amazed, aghast, and astonished judging panel!

'We are Mary-Sue!' I had announced, when we walked into the audition room together. By then we had got our three-legged walking down to a fine art and an exact science. We had been practising for night after night with the giant shoe.

It seemed that the panel hadn't been warned about us and our special unusualness. All three of their jaws dropped when we walked in. Wanda Needlebottom and Trevor Rotter were perched either side of Agatha Staynes at the long table before us. Whereas Agatha was old, flouncy and flowery, Wanda was skinny, mean and trendy as you could get. Trevor was an ex-body-builder-turned-record producer and he was glaring at us over his shades.

113

Agatha Staynes had been in showbiz the longest. She drew upon her many years of professional expertise to enable her to keep calm. 'My dears,' she said. 'You do realise that *Diva Wars* is a talent show for individual performers, and not double acts, don't you?'

Bravely, Eunice and I stood there, arms wrapped around each other's waists; middle feet planted firmly in the giant shoe. 'Yes,' I said. 'We are conjoined twins, and there's nothing in your rule book to say that we can't enter this competition under one single name.'

Agatha went rather pale at this and so did her fellow judges. 'Errr . . . Ehhm . . .' she said, opening and shutting her wrinkly old mouth several times in confusion. 'That's because it's something we have never even thought about.'

'Well, you should have!' I said sharply.

'But we never thought that conjoined twins would be interested in becoming singing sensations or disco divas!'

'Huh!' I shouted. 'Why not?'

Beside me, Eunice was preening prettily and showing off her best side.

'Your sister has got the looks,' said the tactless Trevor. 'But you haven't.'

'Yes, but while we're attached to each other,

we count as the same person! They're my looks as well!'

Agatha Staynes looked fuddled and muddled. She had a face like our mam does when she has a headache coming on. 'We can't argue about this all day . . .'

'I think they should be disqualified,' snapped Trevor, glaring at us from under his mono-brow. 'Who wants to look at them?'

I stuck my tongue out at him. 'You haven't even seen us audition yet,' I said, coolly.

'I don't have to. It will turn my stomach. It's weird. You're weird.'

'Shush, Trevor,' Agatha said.

Then Wanda inched forward and tapped Agatha's arm with one of her skinny fingers. 'This could be a very good thing, you know,' she purred. 'It could be good for the TV ratings. People like stories like this. Triumph over adversity and everything. This could be a real human drama. Winning against the odds.'

Eunice and I exchanged a quick glance. They were getting the message. They would fall for this, hook, line and sinker.

Agatha Staynes sat down heavily. 'All right, then. Perhaps you are right. We should listen to them, anyway. That's the least we can do.'

'So,' I said. 'Can we start, then?'

Agatha nodded. 'Yes, girls. Now – what are you going to sing?'

'"We Are Family", by Sister Sledge.'

'Right. Good. Off you go, then.'

And do you know what?

We wowed them.

All our dance moves looked amazing with three legs. I sang my heart out. Eunice just mimed her part, but we were moving around so much that I'm sure they couldn't even tell. I sang my heart out and it was as if all the disappointments and frustrations of my young life were just melting away. I sang my heart out and I just knew that this was it. This was where I was supposed to be: finding fame here and now, side by side with our Eunice – the two of us strapped together at the ankle.

I sang my heart out and suddenly we were getting the chance to shine.

And we didn't let ourselves down.

We came to a stupendous crescendo.

All three judges were sitting there with their gobs hanging open.

'Well?' I grinned. 'What did you think?'

Even hours afterwards, trundling home in our taxi, I could still hear Agatha Staynes's voice, filled with wonder and quavering excitement.

'My dears ... I think we have witnessed something very, very special ... Today, we three have borne witness to the birth of a brand new megastar in the glittering showbiz firmament!'

Only then had I dared to look at the other two judges. Even though Trevor was known as the hard man of *Diva Wars*, and even though Wanda was known as the Nastiest Mouth on Telly, it was obvious that Eunice and I had made some kind of impression.

'I think you're right, Agatha,' Wanda gasped, in her fake American accent. 'We have glimpsed true greatness – here at our very first audition!'

Agatha, Wanda and Trevor almost never agreed in their verdicts. They also liked to wring every last drop of drama out of the moment – whether destroying someone's dreams for ever, or granting their dearest wishes.

Just then, Eunice and I were relishing every second of that drama.

Chapter Twelve

Eric was sort of right, when he said that the way to success was by making people feel sorry for us. We had seen that straight away, with the looks on the faces of the panel of *Diva Wars*. Agatha Staynes looked like she wanted to gather us up in her arms and smother us in her spangly woolly jumper, covering us with kisses. 'Oh, you poor brave darlings. How you must have suffered! How terrible your conjoined lives must have been!'

Out of the judges, only the terrible Trevor didn't like the look of us – and said so. He was savvy enough to let us through to Round Two, though. He knew the viewing public would adore us.

So Eric was definitely right in most of his predictions about how people would react to us being Siamese twins. What he hadn't reckoned on were the reactions of our fellow contestants . . .

When Round Two began, a little while later, and we had to don our special gigantic shoe once again and prepare for battle – that was when Eunice and Mam and Eric and I all realised how much the other contestants were going to despise us.

'Take no notice,' Mam said when we arrived, doing our expert three-legged walking and wearing matching green catsuits, studded in diamante. We were even wearing – my idea – a mauve feather boa, strung round both our necks. 'They're just jealous of you, that's what. Word has gone round that you two are undoubtedly going to be the winners.'

Eunice tossed her hair and made herself look all haughty. Like a true star, she had the knack of pretending she didn't even know people were staring. I didn't have that knack. I went bright red and stared at the ground, concentrating on our three-legged walking.

We were in the foyer of the Hotel Grandissimo in Brumlington-on-Sea. Eric had driven us down and, during the long journey, we had all been in high spirits. It was like setting off on holiday. The sun was high and bright in the sky, and the boot and roof-rack were packed tight with enough outfits to last us the full week of Round Two. At lunchtime we stopped in a lay-by and ate cheese-and-ham sandwiches Mam had made at six a.m., and we swigged back fizzy pop, watching the cars zooming by on the motorway. We were laughing because Eric had drunk so fast he'd given himself hiccups.

Mam was in an effervescent mood, too. Her sunglasses were perched on top of her head and she looked miles younger and happier than normal. 'Just think, girls. This will be one of the last times we'll have to stop for a packed lunch on the motorway. Soon, it'll all be expensive restaurants for us.'

'And helicopters,' Eunice grinned. 'You said we would travel about in helicopters.'

'How come?' Eric laughed. 'What's the big – *hic* – thing about heli – *hic* – copters?'

Mam shrugged. 'I've just always liked the thought of swooping about out of the clouds and being able to land absolutely anywhere you like.'

'You're crazy,' he said, shaking his head at her fondly. 'Anyway, I *like* having sandwiches and pop – *hic* – in lay-bys. I'd miss doing this if we got too rich and posh to do it any more.'

'When the girls are superstars, we'll be able to do absolutely anything,' Mam said. Then, briskly, she started collecting up all our bits of tin foil and clingfilm and dumped them in the nearby bin. 'Now, girls. While we're here, we're only twenty miles outside of Brumlington-on-Sea. I think you ought to take the opportunity to get yourselves into

120

character. Now, before anyone sees you, you have to turn yourselves into Mary-Sue. You have to put on the big shoe.'

We both pulled faces. 'Already? Do we have to?'

Mam nodded firmly. 'Do as you're told!'

'You see, girls,' Eric said, 'if we're going to go through with this, and deceive everyone, then the story has to be watertight. No one should see you separate and not joined at the foot. You have to become Mary-Sue and stay Mary-Sue for a whole week!'

I groaned and Eunice scowled at him. 'I'm not sure I'm so *KOF KOF* keen on this now,' she said.

'Oh, yes you are, young lady,' snapped Mam. She flung open the car boot and fetched out the box containing the big shoe. 'You two are going to make all our dreams come true.'

And so, over an hour later, we drove into Brumlington-on-Sea. We cooed at the ultra-vivid blue of the sea, and the flashiness of the hotels along the front, and then we got lost in the traffic and eventually found a parking space near enough to the Hotel Grandissimo.

That's when the man standing in a uniform with golden trim opened up the main doors for us, and we really felt like we had arrived in a world of glamour and poshness. We walked into the hotel foyer, and were immediately aware of all these eyes upon us.

Showbiz brats! Singing pop tarts! Kids in sequins, spangles, ruffles and make-up! It seemed like there were hundreds of them in that foyer. Girls with flinty, hostile eyes, standing there with their doting dads and grandmas, pushy mums and aunties. All of them were desperate to be divas. All of them were mad keen to win. They would stop at nothing to get through to the quarter-finals. At the end of this week of Round Two, only ten potential divas would be left. So ... forty had to be eliminated during this coming week.

That was why it was so tense inside the Hotel Grandissimo. It was buzzing with cut-throat ambition. It was bristling with glitzy tension. The very air was flammable as cheap hairspray.

Mam and Eric were talking with the toffee-nosed receptionist, sorting out our rooms. There was some confusion over Eunice and my sleeping arrangements. 'Of course they will need a double bed. They can't exactly have twin beds, can they? They're conjoined twins! What do you want them to do, hang their poor middle foot out between the beds?' Mam was getting shrill and the receptionist was growing flustered and, all around us, I was aware of the other contestants – all forty-nine of them, plus their families – muttering and commenting and mithering on.

'It's hardly fair, is it?'

'Someone should complain . . .'

'I already have. I've phoned the producer, emailed the executive producer, and I've harangued the TV company's board of directors in the street! I've even penned a stiff missive to Agatha Staynes herself . . .'

'It stands to reason, doesn't it? It shouldn't be allowed!'

'Two heads are better than one, after all, aren't they? Hahahaha!'

'It's just a gimmick. A cheap, rotten gimmick!'

Just when it seemed that the crowd was turning its nastiest, and just when I felt most like wrenching my foot free of the giant shoe and abandoning the whole, silly charade, Eunice did something very strange. Something she had never done before. I mean, I've already said – usually, she's a complete cow, right? Well, right then she took hold of my hand and gave it a tight, reassuring squeeze. It was our middle hands, so nobody else could see. She didn't have to do it. I was amazed at her.

The mutters and murmurs were getting worse, all around us.

'That little one . . . – well! Just look at her! What does she look like?'

'A monkey in a catsuit!'

'They should be in a circus, or a freak show! Not *Diva Wars*! *Diva Wars* is only for the most special, most beautiful little girls – like my Angelica . . .'

Eunice squeezed my hand once more and I squeezed back. Suddenly it seemed okay. We were a team. We were a double act! We didn't have to be scared of that skinny, glittery, nasty-mouthed lot!

Then Mam whirled around, smiling. 'That's that all sorted out!' she announced. 'They've given us a whole suite of rooms at the very top!'

'A suite!' Eric gasped.

Eunice and I weren't quite sure what a suite was exactly, but it sounded very grand, so we gasped as well.

Minutes later, we stepped out of the plush lift into a luxurious corridor at the very top of the Hotel Grandissimo. The porter unlocked our door for us and we struggled in with all our many bags of showbiz gear. That was when we realised what a suite was. It was like a whole house! All these rooms, all to ourselves, right at the top of the hotel. Someone had sent us gorgeous pink lilies; a dozen vases of them, sprouting out on the side tables and coffee tables and on top of the super-duper

TV and hi-fi. There were fat comfy sofas and a vast picture window overlooking the brilliant sea.

'Oo-er,' said Eric. 'This is the high life, all right! Isn't it, girls?'

Eunice and I went pacing about, three-leggedly exploring all the many rooms of our suite. We were both trembling with excitement. Could it be true? Everything Mam had always promised – was it really possible?

We heard the porter say to our mam: 'Aren't they just adorable? And so brave! So special! They don't half deserve to win, they do!'

Mam thanked him and gave him a tip. Then she turned to us.

'Right, girls! There's to be no relaxing! No luxuriating in all this fabulous splendour! There'll be plenty of time for that later on. Now it's time – to get rehearsing!'

Chapter Thirteen

It was the most exhausting week of our lives.

It was okay for Mam and Eric. It turned out that they didn't have to do very much at all. They used the hotel swimming pool and jacuzzi, and they sat in the bar, and strolled up and down the promenade together. They even went to the fair and came back with a green fluffy duck Eric had won chucking coconuts. They were having a proper holiday together!

The only thing they had to do was be filmed by the TV crew of *Diva Wars* a couple of times. Mam would say things like, 'Of course I am terribly, terribly proud of my girls. They have had to overcome so much prejudice and so many difficulties in their young and precious lives. They work so hard. They rehearse day and night until they are absolutely perfect.'

For this particular interview, the four of us were sitting on the largest, squashiest sofa in our suite.

Eunice and I were in the middle, with our shared foot and giant shoe propped up on the coffee table, displaying itself prominently for the cameras. We were smiling angelically, just as we had practised.

'And what about your daddy?' said the TV interviewer suddenly. He was crouching on the carpet with his microphone, which he pushed into Eric's startled face. 'I suppose you're very proud of your daughters, aren't you?'

'Er, um,' said Eric, flustered. 'I'm proud, but I'm afraid that I'm not . . . Um . . .'

Mam broke in. 'He's over the moon. He's cock-a-hoop. He couldn't be prouder of them.'

The TV man grinned and we thought that was the end of the interview. We all sat back, relaxing now. Then he asked Mam, 'But really, what do you think about all these mutterings and complaints?'

'What about?' Mam frowned.

'Some of the other contestants – they're complaining to the TV company and the presenters that it's not fair that Mary-Sue is allowed to join in this competition for individual performers.' The TV man looked very solemn, and I saw that they were still recording us. 'They want to get Mary-Sue disqualified.'

'What?' cried Mam. 'That's just sheer discrimination! What are my daughters supposed to do? Join

127

a contest for groups? Be a double act, when they're joined at the foot?'

'It's just what some of the other mothers are saying,' shrugged the TV man.

'They're being spiteful,' Mam raged, 'because they know that we are going to win! They might as well hand over the prizes right now and save us all the bother!'

Mam didn't know they were still quietly filming her. It was this clip, of her ranting and raving about how we were definitely going to win, that got repeated on all the shows and even on the news. It stirred up the other contestants further and made the atmosphere stickier than ever!

That was still fairly early in our week at the Hotel Grandissimo.

Eunice and I had been having singing practice and dancing practice and talking-to-the-cameras practice for hours and hours every day. 'It's like being in the army,' Eunice had moaned, flopping down on our shared bed at the end of the third day.

'Yeah,' I said, being yanked down beside her. 'An army where you have to wear loads of make-up and hairspray and legwarmers and dance about to "Yes Sir, I Can Boogie". That kind of army.'

'You know what I mean,' Eunice grumped.

I nodded. Old Eunice hadn't been too bad this

week, actually. It was as if, now we were faced with the sometimes open hostility of the other *Diva* wannabes, we had to stick together and she had realised that. We had to present a united front. Mind, it was still murder having to stay tied to her all the time and to share a bed with her too! She might have the face of an angel, but she got terrible wind. Eunice pumped under the duvet all night long, just about gassing me. And it's *really* horrible being tied at the foot to another person when they have to go to the loo. There was no way round it, if we wanted to keep our pretence up. 'This is just one of those things,' Mam said. 'If you two are serious about wanting the fame and the fortune, then there are sacrifices you just have to make.'

And there was Mam, propping up the Bar Galactica each night with Eric and having a whale of a time. Even up in our suite, Eunice and I could hear the thud-thud-thudding of the disco down in the Hotel Grandissimo's basement. All the contestants' parents seemed to be down there each night, dancing away like teenagers – cavorting with each other – what a revolting thought! And meanwhile their kids were getting their much-needed rest. We needed all the energy we could get, ready for our dance classes and our singing lessons and all the prancing about and the 'LLALALALALA's and the 'MEMEMEMEMEEEE's that we had to get through every day.

Fifty-one potential divas were singing their hearts out and boogieing like mad on the sprung floor of the hotel's grand ballroom. Fifty-one divas were staring at themselves in giant mirrors and honing their performances to perfection. Fifty-one of us were glancing slyly sideways and keeping careful tabs on the opposition. Is she prettier than I am? they were thinking. Thinner and more curvy? Does she hit more of the notes than I do? Sustain her vibrato longer? Ha! Look at her! She's rubbish! What's she even doing here? I'm the best. I'm surely the best. There's no one here as good as me . . .

Evelina Semolina was easily the best of all the rest. Whatever we might have thought of her – that she was a simpering, saccharine fool – didn't matter beside her sheer talent. It turned out she could do just about everything. Sing and dance in any style required. She had been a stage-school brat since the age of two and it really showed.

She hated Eunice and I at first glance. She thought we were common and freakish, and wasted no time in telling us.

'You shouldn't be here,' she sneered, whenever she danced close to us. 'You should be in the circus! The zoo!'

Eunice said something very rude to her that time, and Evelina blushed deeply. Nasty she might be, but she was still very ladylike.

We were taught to smile and simper, just like Evelina, as we danced and sang round the ballroom. But inside, all of us were thinking nasty, competitive, evil and jealous thoughts.

You could just about hear those thoughts, thrumming enviously on the hot and sweaty air. I could hear them coming out of Eunice too, as if we really *were* joined as a single body. I wasn't as bothered, really. I mean, yes, it would be nice to win *Diva Wars*, because the prizes were so fabby and stellar. It was worth aiming for that. But I wasn't going to kill myself if we didn't win. I didn't take it to heart like some of them!

During that week, the judges passed amongst us, whittling us down from fifty-one.

It was an extremely gruesome sight!

Agatha Staynes, Wanda Needlebottom and Trevor Rotter came drifting through the hotel like sharks out hunting at the bottom of the sea. They wove their way through the rehearsals in the Grand Ballroom, their eyes squinched up in expert concentration. Everyone's heart jumped when they hoved into view and, at that moment, everyone started working just that bit harder.

'Push yourselves, girls!' screeched the dance tutor. 'Give it one hundred and ten per cent! You too, Mary-Sue! In fact, you should give it two hundred and twenty per cent!'

The two of us blushed at this and our dance moves faltered. I blamed nerves and the extra-large legwarmer over our extra-large shoe. Luckily, the judges didn't notice our missed steps. They were moving stealthily through the room elsewhere, and tapping certain mini-divas on the shoulder. It was like the angels of death hovering about the place.

We all knew what that meant, when you got tapped on the shoulder.

We had been warned. We knew what you had to do. You were to stop what you were doing immediately. There were to be no tears, no strops, no recriminations. You were supposed to just stop what you were doing and leave the rehearsal room. Then you were to go back to your room in the Hotel Grandissimo and pack your bags. You were out of the contest! That's how it happened. It was supposed to cause a minimum of fuss – but, of course, what happened was just terrible. People screamed! They shrieked and bawled! We saw one girl collapse onto the wooden floor like she was having a fit. She was thrashing around and beating the floorboards with her fists. Then she was grabbing hold of Agatha Staynes's legs and begging, begging to be allowed to stay in the competition. But Agatha – mumsy and flowery though she was – wouldn't listen to a word of it. All three judges were resolute. They had to be professional and heartless. They had to be! How else were they going to discover the best of the very best?

So that week, we got quite used to it. Bopping and boogieing and singing along, vaguely aware that these showbiz angels of death were watching our every move and looking for flaws and mistakes. We even got used to the noise when some poor hapless soul got that sudden tap on the shoulder.

'NOOOOOO! NOoooOOOOooooOOOO! You can't! You can't chuck me out!'

'Mmuuummmyyyy! AAAAaaaggghhhh!!!!!'

Eunice even caught my eye on a couple of these occasions and started to laugh. I shook my head at her. We couldn't afford to gloat, or to get complacent. Eunice had been right at the start of the week – it was indeed like being in the army. It was just like being at war. We couldn't let our guard down for even a second.

We were dancing to an ancient song by Abba on the Thursday afternoon and I was just thinking along these lines, counting our steps – one, two THREE ... one, two, THREE – and kicking our big shoe into the air on every THREE, and that was when IT happened.

Evelina Semolina came dancing past us, grinning like crazy. She was light as a feather, but her feet were hard from all the ballet lessons she'd taken since the age of two. We didn't see it coming but, as she whirled past us, she lashed out with one of her deadly feet and caught us right on the shins of our middle legs.

We yelled out in pain. Loud as anything. Evelina went waltzing off, innocent as you like. Eunice said a very rude word and I fell over.

A terrible shock went through me. A terrible shock went through the two of us.

We had stopped dancing!

Two meaty palms landed on our shoulders!

And all of a sudden Trevor Rotter was grinning down at us both!

'That's it, girls, you can stop dancing now,' he said, chuckling for the benefit of the cameras. 'That wasn't a very elegant series of moves, was it? Oh dear, no. I'm afraid you leave me with no alternative! You are now, as of this moment, officially rejected! Both of you!'

Chapter Fourteen

For several moments Eunice and I were in complete shock. It's a horrible feeling. A falling to earth with a big fat bump. One minute you're dancing around and grinning like an idiot, just like they're teaching you to – and then it's tap-tap-tap on your shoulder.

We were led out of the hot, pounding disco heat of the ballroom. Eunice and I gallumphed out of there, dragging our three feet along and blushing with absolute shame. We just knew that all the other divas were watching us gleefully. They were glad we were gone. Trevor Rotter was escorting us, his hand still firmly on Eunice's shoulder. She looked ready to whip her head round like an evil alien in a film and tear his whole arm off in her slavering jaws. He was just so smug.

Eunice and I behaved very well, though. We didn't go into a whole palaver like others had done. We didn't throw some mega-strop all over the place. We hung our heads and walked calmly out of the room. We knew we had to be dignified for being on telly. There was no use causing a commotion, once you'd been kicked out.

'*Kicked out? Disqualified? Sent home?!*'

Of course, Mam took the news much harder than we did. Eric said she had just about choked on her cocktail in the Bar Galactica, where the two of them had been idling the afternoon away. With Eric at her heels, she came dashing out of that gaudy, sci-fi themed bar and saw us there in the foyer, standing with Trevor Rotter, and being filmed in our misery.

'Oh no,' I whispered to Eunice. 'Look. Mam's been told.'

She came thundering towards us through the plush foyer, scattering potted plants and pouffes and old-age pensioners. 'How could you?' she yelled, right into Trevor's face. She stood in front of him, staring into his startled mug. We had to admire her courage. Trevor Rotter was as big as an ice-cream van and he wasn't known for his sensitivity. He was rippling with muscles, but our mam didn't care. She'd had several space-age-type cocktails in the Bar Galactica and there was no holding her, even though Eric made a slight attempt to prevent her using actual physical violence on the gloating Rotter.

'Who are you, to take my daughters' dreams and stamp on them? What kind of man are you? What kind of *manager* are you, not to see their talent and their showbiz potential? You must be loopy! You must be out of your mind!'

Trevor was very calm. 'I am perfectly sane and in possession of all my showbiz faculties, Mrs Gutteridge. And I have disqualified your daughters because I don't think they are good enough. End of story.'

Mam went quiet and very still. When she spoke again, her voice was very deliberate. Her teeth were grinding together like rocks. '*You – don't – think – my – daughters – are – good – enough?*'

'Mrs Gutteridge,' he sighed. 'We are here in this ghastly town, in order to find the very best of the best. You have seen the wealth of talent here. You have seen how marvellous some of these girls are. I am afraid your girls don't quite cut the showbiz mustard. So I am sending them home. I'm sorry.'

'You fat *pig*,' Mam said.

'What?'

'You heard! You *jumped-up drongo*! You *peahead*! You *creep*! You *slimeball*!'

'Hey, now, Marjorie,' Eric tried to break in. 'Dignity, remember, love. You're being filmed, remember.'

'I don't care,' Mam yelled. 'This *utter creep* is disqualifying my poor, talented Siamese daughters! He doesn't care! He's got no heart!' She was beating her fists on Trevor Rotter's massive chest. He took gentle hold of her wrists and stopped her.

'All I care about is finding the biggest and best diva in the country,' he said. 'My job is to whittle down the rubbish and leave the best behind. And the best ain't Mary-Sue.'

And that, it seemed, was an end to it.

Eunice and I looked at each other. 'KOFKOF-KOF,' went Eunice.

Until then, it hadn't really, completely sunk in.

We were being sent home! We had failed!

Except . . .

Except that Agatha Staynes was as furious as our mam.

The TV crew told Agatha what had happened, the moment she returned from her hair appointment at Salon Berthold at 5.30 p.m. It being her afternoon off, she had spent her time being primped and titivated, and she arrived back at the Hotel Grandissimo with her hair frosted lime-green, all newly set in a big candyfloss perm. When they told her what Trevor Rotter had done during her absence, she bellowed and seethed and looked just about ready to rip that new hairdo right off her own head.

'The very moment my back is turned! He's done this on purpose, just to spite me! Trevor never, ever thought Mary-Sue should be allowed into this contest. He's always been against the poor thing. He's got his own favourites. He wants Evelina Semolina to win, just because he fancies her mother. I know what he's up to! Well, he won't get away with it. Those poor girls. Those poor conjoined girls!'

Agatha made a great show for the cameras, shaking her fists and kicking up a proper storm of protest on our account. Didn't I tell you they loved milking all the drama on *Diva Wars*? They always play it up melodramatically for the viewers at home – that's why we loved the show so much. But now it was different. Eunice and I were right in the thick of it.

'It's like being in the eye of the hurricane,' Eric said dolefully. He was sitting on the squashy sofa and Mam was pacing up and down, as she had done for over an hour.

'That's good,' she said. 'That's a good thing to say, when they interview you. You could say that, all around there's the hurricane of emotion and tears – all the ambition and tragedy and everything – and here, up in our luxurious suite, it's like the still, silent eye of the hurricane. We are the cause of all the drama. And here sit two very disappointed and heartbroken, very tragic twins. All of their dreams shattered by a nasty, slimy pig of a man.'

Eric sighed. 'It's been just like a ... like an emotional roller-coaster.'

'That's brilliant!' Mam burst out. 'I could say that line when they interview us. I could say – it's all been ups and downs. We have had some wonderful highs, when we just knew that the girls would have their genius discovered and rewarded. But then we've also had terrible, dreadful lows as well – just like a roller-coaster, literally like a roller-coaster – and now we've come to the end of the line ...' Mam started sobbing again, covering her face with one hand and waving the imaginary camera away with the other.

Eunice jumped to her feet, crossly. Naturally, I was dragged to my feet, too.

'Will you two just stop coming out with bloody awful *KOF KOF KOF* clichés?' she shouted.

'What?' Mam stared at her.

'You! You're wallowing! You're saying the same old things that everyone says! Roller-coasters! Emotional hurricanes! Think of something new to say, why don't you? And anyway – aren't you sick of giving interviews by now? *KOF KOF.* You must have given about thirty this week already. All about the sacrifices you've made to enable your daughters to become stars . . . about the long journey and the *KOF* hardships you've endured along the way . . .'

Mam looked stung. 'Well, it's true. I've only told the truth, haven't I?'

Eunice screeched: 'BUT IT'S NOT ABOUT YOU!'

Everyone went quiet.

'It's about *us*,' Eunice said, in the ringing silence. 'It's about me and Helen and how . . . how we are losers. We've lost this, now. We haven't even made it through to the quarter-finals. We've *KOF* failed again and that's all there is to it. *KOF KOF.*'

Eric shuffled forward. 'Hey, hey . . . your mam was just disappointed, and being fierce on your behalf. She's like a lioness with her cubs. She just wants the best for you two. You know that . . .'

Eunice was shaking her head. 'No, Eric. You don't understand. You hardly *KOF* understand anything. Mam wants it for herself. Just herself.'

Eric didn't reply to that. What could he say? He just looked at Mam. We all looked at Mam. And suddenly all the fight had gone out of her. She turned and walked into her bedroom and closed the door behind her.

Eric stared at us two girls very sadly. 'Best leave her be for now.' He looked awkward, standing there in the middle of our suite. I wondered vaguely when we would have to go. Straight after the interviews this evening? Would they let us stay another night? Eric must have been thinking along similar lines because he said, 'I'll help the two of you to pack up your showbiz gear.'

Chapter Fifteen

It's strange to think of it now, but by the time we had left the Hotel Grandissimo and Brumlington-on-Sea, and by the time we had returned home and were back in our normal lives, not a single episode of *Diva Wars* had yet been broadcast. For some time it had been right at the forefront of our minds. Even I had been obsessed, letting that daft competition take over everything else in my head. But to the rest of the country, *Diva Wars* was just a few adverts that showed up between other programmes: building up to the first episode, which would be on two Saturdays after our return.

It wouldn't be right to say that, by then, we were completely over our disappointment at being booted out. That wouldn't be right at all. Poor Mam spent a few whole days lying in bed and sobbing. Eric started looking after us and ordering takeaways for us. He hardly ever went home now to Broad Bottom and The Dirty Duck. He had just about moved in with us, and that kind of proved how much he thought of us – he must even love us, I remember thinking – because round ours was a pretty miserable place to be during those weeks. Where had all the optimism and happiness gone? That holiday feeling we'd had in the car, on the drive to Brumlington-on-Sea? That marvellous luxurious feeling of staying in the hotel suite? All those great feelings had melted away overnight. All it took was that tap-tap-tap on our shoulder . . .

Eunice was mutinous. She sat in our bedroom, doing her hair at her dressing table, combing it out savagely. 'I don't see why Mam's like she is,' she groused. 'It should be us refusing to get out of bed. It should be us as depressed as that. But we've got to go to school! We don't get to stay in, like she does.'

I was sitting on my bed. 'You know what she's like,' I said. 'She takes it all to heart. Our rejection is her rejection. She takes it all very personally.'

'So do I! I wanted to win, as well!'

I admitted, 'So did I. By the time we were there, I was really into it.' I smiled. 'It was great, wasn't it?'

Eunice finished putting bobbles in her plaited hair. 'Well, there's no use going over it all now. There'll be plenty of time for that, when they start showing the TV programme.'

'It'll be weird, seeing ourselves on there . . .'

144

She nodded. 'It'll be like – watching it, and egging ourselves on. And, even though we know what happened, and that we got chucked out . . . it'll be like, by wishing hard enough, we'll be able to change the outcome . . .'

'I know what you mean,' I said. 'Stupid, isn't it? Like wishing hard enough ever made any difference.'

'I hate Trevor Rotter,' Eunice glowered.

'The others were okay, though, and *some* of the contestants were nice.'

Eunice sighed. 'Others were cows, though. If that Evelina Semolina wins, I think I'll absolutely kill myself.'

There was something about the savage serious-ness of the way Eunice said that, that made me laugh out loud. For a second Eunice glared at me, then she started laughing as well. 'I sound like Mam!' she gasped. 'I'm going showbiz crazy, like her!' We carried on laughing until Mam started knocking on the wall between our rooms. She was having yet another lie-down, and our laughter was disturbing her.

What have they got to laugh about? she would be thinking. They're failed divas! They're useless singing non-sensations! How come they can laugh about it?

That's what poor Mam would be thinking.

145

'Let's go downstairs,' I said. 'Eric's phoning for a takeaway. Thai, I think.'

'Woo-ooo,' said Eunice. 'Another takeaway! I think I'm getting to think Eric's okay, you know.'

Eunice was really changing! As we went downstairs, I found myself thinking, Eunice has transformed herself into a decent human being!

In the kitchen Eric had his mobile in one hand and the Thai takeaway menu in the other.

'Girls, your mam's just phoned and asked if you can keep the noise of your laughter down.' He looked a bit strained and pale. 'She says she's too upset to come down to eat this evening.'

'What?!' Eunice laughed. 'You mean, she rang you from her bedroom upstairs, to tell us, who were in the room next door, to pipe down?'

Eric nodded, biting his lip.

'She's gone bananas!' Eunice cried. She raised her voice deliberately, shouting at the artex sculpted ceiling, and hoping that Mam would hear her in the bedroom above. 'She's crazy! She wants locking up! It was only a TV show!'

'Sssh, now, Eunice,' Eric stammered. 'You know how she is.'

'She's loopy!' Eunice shouted. 'It should be us who's upset! Not her!'

146

'Let's order a banquet for eight,' Eric said, with false cheeriness. 'Thai food never quite fills you up, does it?' He grinned down at me, as I hoisted myself up on a kitchen stool.

'Okay,' I said. 'A banquet for eight. So long as we have battered prawns.'

We were willing life to go back to normal. If only Mam could pull herself out of this depressive funk, and we could forget all about our humiliation at the Hotel Grandissimo. I didn't want any more sleepless nights wondering: was it my voice? Was I really not good enough? Didn't I try hard enough? Was it our dancing? Was it our looks? You could torture yourself, turning these thoughts over and over in your mind. You could worry yourself down to nothing, if you kept at it too long. Well, I was a dwarf and I couldn't afford to worry great lumps of myself away. I was going to stop thinking about *Diva Wars*, and that was an end to the matter. I was glad and relieved we were home and out of that glittery rat race. I was glad to be normal, with the tension off. And I was glad to be just myself, and not yoked to my sister any more. No more pretending! No more lies!

'Come on then, girls,' Eric said. 'We've still got another twelve main dishes to choose from the menu . . .'

147

I watched Eunice smile at Eric. So, she really was warming to him. It was just as well. He was more or less a permanent fixture in our lives now.

It was then I noticed the TV guide on the kitchen bench. Next week's telly, starting Saturday. *Diva Wars* all over the cover: Agatha Staynes, Wanda Needlebottom and Trevor Rotter, all three of them dolled up and glamorous, standing in a galaxy of stars, holding up the trophy in the shape of a golden microphone.

'Ah,' said Eric, noticing that I'd seen the mag. 'Well, we don't have to watch it, do we?'

'Whaaat?!' I couldn't believe him. 'Of course we have to watch it! We were fantastic! We have to tape it, and keep it on for ever!'

Saturday night was going to be celebratory. That's what we decided. Eric, Eunice and I even decided that we were going to have home-cooked food for once. We took a trip into town and stocked up on brilliant things like tacos and fajitas and chilli sauce and everything Mexican we could find.

'Why a Mexican theme?' Eunice asked, as we went up and down the supermarket aisles, pushing the trolley along together. 'What's that got to do with *Diva Wars?*'

'Ah,' said Eric. 'Our Helen wants to be a travel

agent, doesn't she? She has to know about exotic food from all over the world, doesn't she?'

I grinned at that. Someone had remembered! Someone had actually taken my travel-agent ambition seriously!

Mexican food is quite fiddly. It's all about making up hot little parcels of cheese and chilli and shredded lettuce and tomato. Everything gets deliciously slathered in sour cream and spicy salsa. It took the three of us hours, late on Saturday afternoon, to get our feast organised and our trays of nibbles hissing and spitting in the oven. Eric had gone through his CDs and found us suitable, salsa-type music. We were singing along happily, even though we didn't know the words. It was the kind of singing you do when you don't care if anyone's listening.

Eunice looked up from the salad she was tossing and gasped.

Mam was standing in the kitchen doorway, all dressed and done up.

'Mam! You've come down!'

She had been up in her room for over a week. She grinned weakly at the welcome we gave her, hugging her and kissing her, and getting sour cream and chilli on her. She had washed and combed her hair, and put on a new, very soft woollen jumper

149

Eric had recently bought her. She had even put on a bit of make-up.

'You've come down to watch the show with us,' smiled Eric approvingly. He flung open the oven door to check on his chimichangas.

'I've come to see what a mess you're making of my kitchen,' she said, glancing around. 'Who's going to clear this lot up?'

'Never mind about that now,' he said, and set to mixing up Margaritas for the two of them. Mam soon started looking less edgy and strained.

'I've a surprise, girls,' Eric said, as we took a pause for fizzy orange at the end of all our culinary labours.

'A surprise?' Eunice narrowed her eyes. Since the *Teen Sensation* debacle at the shopping mall, she'd gone right off surprises of all sorts.

A taxi was arriving outside our house.

'*That's* our surprise?' Eunice asked. Then she looked sorry for sounding sarcastic.

Eric's mam, Marlene, was being helped out of the taxi by her driver. She was in a very glamorous evening gown, all tassels and silver glitter. Her hair was up in a beehive and she was rattling with all her very best jewellery.

'Girls! Girls!' she cried, coming down our garden path and holding out her tiny arms in welcome.

She hurtled towards us, tactfully not noticing the scrubby muddy mess of our back garden. We went out to greet her and she hugged us fiercely hard.

'Ah, never mind, never mind,' she said, patting our backs. Eunice really had to crouch to be hugged by her. 'Those judges can't have had their heads screwed on right, could they? Fancy, not being able to recognise your talent!' She patted us fondly, sighing. 'Ah, there, there. A little bit of failure is good for the soul, you know. A performer has to learn how to take hard knocks. That's what being an artiste is all about. And do you know – all that crushing and pounding and being squashed into nothing, that's how rare jewels are made, you know. Deep under the earth, that's how they get pummelled into brilliant being.'

'Er ... right,' Eunice said, fed up at being squashed and cuddled out in our garden. She pulled herself free of Marlene and led the way back into our wonderfully Mexican-smelling kitchen.

I was keener on Marlene's sympathy and words of wisdom. We had already had that metaphor about the jewels under the earth being made by crushing and squashing. She had said that over the phone to us a couple of times since our return from Brumlington-on-Sea. We hadn't seen her to have it said in the flesh, yet. Now she was coming out with all her greatest showbiz consolation phrases. 'It's a long hard ladder up to the land of stardom,' she sighed, standing in our kitchen, and staring about with gleaming, interested eyes. 'And lots of the rungs have dropped off!'

You got the feeling that Marlene had said all of these things many times before. She had been in showbiz for a long, long time, I supposed, and she had seen as much as there was to see.

'Stardom is like taking a rocket to the moon,' she said. 'Sometimes you blow up before you get there.'

I hoped her showbiz similes wouldn't go on all night.

'Let's go through to the lounge,' Eric said brightly. 'Then we can start serving up supper and get the telly on ready.'

'Lovely home you've got here, Marjorie,' Marlene said to Mam. 'You've made it really lovely, considering you haven't been here long.'

'We've been really busy!' Mam said, defensively. 'There hasn't been time to redecorate, or to empty out all the packing crates or anything.'

'I didn't mean that,' Marlene said. 'I wasn't being sarcastic.'

'Hmm,' said Mam, showing her into the kitchen. It was true, Mam often thought people were being saracastic when they weren't. I was starting to see how defensive and jumpy she was – all the time! With everyone! Even us! And I swore to myself that I would never be like that.

'Mmm, Mexican food, lovely,' said Marlene, settling onto the settee. 'It might give my delicate tummy a bit of gyp, but never mind. I can see you've gone to a lot of effort! Lovely!'

Eric was fiddling with the TV remote. He had made some further alterations to our digi-box tuning and now we had more channels and more complications than ever.

'Oh, hurry up, Eric, it can't be that hard to find,' Mam said impatiently, handing round plates. 'It'll be starting any minute now! We can't miss it!'

'Aha!' he said, as he flashed onto the right channel.

'Oooh! Good luck, girls!' Marlene said, as if it was all happening live, and as if we didn't already know the awful outcome.

But somehow, that didn't matter now.

Eunice and I exchanged a glance as the music crashed in, and the screen exploded into the familiar, glitzy and tacky title sequence. A new season of *Diva Wars* was beginning! And we – us two! – were actually part of it!

Chapter Sixteen

I watched our bit from behind a cushion. I just about smothered myself into unconsciousness. I nearly choked on the tassels, I was pushing it so hard into my face when I knew it was us coming on the telly.

I hadn't expected to be embarrassed!

For a full hour the show concentrated on the auditioning process, as the three judges went to each major city in the country and hundreds of wannabes flooded into the hotels where the auditions were held.

'Look at them all,' Eunice said, amazed. 'There are thousands of them. You don't realise how many put themselves in for it . . .'

Marlene, who was sitting on the settee between the two of us, reached over and patted her hand. 'There you are, you see? That's how many people you've beaten, just by getting through to the next round!'

'Hmm,' said Eunice, crunching into a taco.

'Showbiz is a bit like horse-racing—' said Marlene, and Mam went, 'SSSSsssshh!' abruptly, because the cameras were in our city suddenly, panning along the queue outside the hotel very early in the morning.

'I think I saw us!' Mam cried out. 'I think I got a glimpse of Eric! He was facing the wrong way . . .'

We all laughed at that, remembering how, when the camera crew had passed along by the queue and we were all supposed to wave, Eric had been facing the wrong way but waved like mad anyway. He kept doing things, I realised, to make himself look daft, just to take our nerves away.

Then they started showing the actual auditions. Usually when we were watching this show as mere members of the public and not as contestants, we loved to see the auditions. They could be really funny. This was when the sharp-witted cruelty and rudeness of the panel even became entertaining. True to form, Trevor Rotter and Wanda Needle-bottom said some needlessly horrible and cruel things to the people who came trooping in.

'Well, it was true,' Eunice said. 'She *did* have a mouth like a cat's bum! *And* she couldn't sing a single note! She needed to be told!'

'And she couldn't dance at all,' Eric said thoughtfully.

'And that one didn't try enough! She looked like she couldn't be bothered,' sighed Marlene.

'I think she was very nervous,' Mam said, sipping her Margarita.

'Nervous!' cried Marlene. 'You can't afford the luxury of nervousness. Not in showbiz! You have to get out there and grab the bull by both horns. Showbiz is like riding a wild untamed horse—'

'I thought it was like a bull?' Mam said. 'Or a ladder, wasn't it? Or was it a rocket going to the moon?'

Ooops, I thought. Mam's getting sarcastic.

'Look!' Eunice screeched. '*It's US!!!*'

And that was when I grabbed the cushion at my back and just about suffocated myself with it. I couldn't bear seeing myself on the telly. On we came, me and Eunice, tethered together at the foot by our huge and specially-made shoe!

I hid myself away and listened carefully. Everyone else in the front room fell silent while we were on.

I listened to the whole thing unfold. The way I introduced us. Our alias. My lies. More lies. Our subterfuge. The conversation with the judges. Our being allowed to sing at last.

156

Our – my – wonderful singing.

I heard it all. And the confusion and the bewilderment of the judges. Then, Agatha Staynes's rhapsodising about our talent! And, even though I couldn't bring myself to actually look at the screen, I could imagine our faces on there, glowing with excitement and pride and triumph, at being told that we were being put through to Round Two. My Mexican-food-filled stomach was turning over in queasy sympathy at the memory of that moment.

It had been brilliant! I had tried to forget it. For the good of my sanity, I had tried to forget what it had felt like, to win through in that way. To feel a success! To feel like I was a step closer to stardom ... And now all those intense and dazzling sensations were back. They came flooding back as we sat there on the settee.

'Siamese twins!' I heard Trevor Rotter saying. 'That's ridiculous. That's cheating. They should count as two people, not one.'

'There's nothing in the rules, Trevor,' Agatha was telling him firmly. 'And I think they're marvellous. They're disco geniuses! Did you see them dancing on their three legs? What skill!'

And then there was a commercial break.

The adverts came on loudly and Eric lowered the volume.

Still it was very quiet in our living room. How come? Did the others think we were terrible? Had we done something wrong?

Warily, I lowered the cushion from over my face.

Mam, Eric and Eunice were all staring at Marlene.

At first I thought Eric's tiny mother was having a heart attack. She was sitting bolt upright with a very strange, set expression on her face.

'Mam?' prompted Eric worriedly. 'What is it? You don't look right . . .'

Her gimlet eyes flicked around the room. She looked at all of us and I suddenly realised what her expression was. It was disgust! Dismay! Disappointment!

She slid off the settee and onto the floor. She went to pick up her overcoat and turned to glare up at us all with what felt like utter contempt.

'How dare you?' Marlene said at last, in a very calm, restrained voice. You could tell that she was holding her fury back inside, though. 'How dare you . . . *cheat?*'

'What?' said Mam.

'Oh no,' Eric gulped.

'How were they cheating?' Mam cried. 'How was that cheating?'

Marlene started to raise her voice. Her face

was turning a livid fuchsia colour. 'You had your daughters pretend to be joined at the foot! You had them go round pretending to be conjoined twins! Of course that's cheating!'

'I don't see how,' said Mam. 'It's just making the best of a bad lot. All's fair in love and showbiz, isn't it?'

'No, it is not!' Marlene thundered. 'Showbiz is an extremely important affair! And so is artistic integrity! If you can't make it on your own, then you can't cheat your way into stardom! It has to be fair and above board!' She swung round on Eric. 'No good will come of this, you mark my words. How could you let them go ahead with this, Eric? You should have stopped them!'

'It's all over now, anyway, Mam,' he said. 'They're out of the competition. There's no harm done.'

She flung her arm out towards the TV. 'No harm done, he says! But they've been on the telly! Lying through their teeth and saying they've got something wrong with them that patently isn't true! Oh, girls . . . I'd have expected more from you. You're only young, but I thought you had more sense. It was all your mother's idea, wasn't it? She'll stop at nothing. I've seen the sort before—'

'I BEG YOUR PARDON!' Mam bellowed.

'WHAT DID YOU SAY, YOU MINUSCULE WITCH?'

'I don't want to stay here a moment longer,' said Marlene, fussily doing up all the buttons on her coat. She ignored Mam and hurried into the kitchen. 'I don't want to be around liars and fraudulent Siamese twins. Get your car keys and your coat, Eric. I'm going back to Broad Bottom. I wish I'd never come now.'

Mam rocketed after her into the kitchen. Then Eunice was on her feet. 'Quick! She'll scrag her!'

We hurried after the grown-ups, and found that, in the kitchen, amongst all the Mexican debris, Eric was having to force his mam and our mam apart. They looked like they wanted to rip each other to shreds.

'She's a lousy drunk,' Marlene was shouting. 'She's hard as nails! She's ruthless!'

'You're jealous!' Mam spat back at her. 'Just because you never made it. You're just jealous of my girls!'

'You can't fake stardom!' Marlene snarled. 'You can't cheat and lie your way to the top!'

'Yes you can! Of course you can!' Mam gave a near-hysterical laugh. 'What do you think everyone else does, eh? You moronic old hag! You just don't understand anything! You never made it! You never became a star! Not a *big* star! Not a *proper* star! Not a star that anyone still remembers! Don't you go telling us what's right and what's wrong!'

'I think you'd better go, Mam,' Eric said.

Marlene looked up at her son. Her mascara was running down her face. 'You're coming with me. And you're not stepping foot in this woman's house again. Her kids are all right, but she's crazy! She's evil!'

Eric was shaking his head. He opened the kitchen door for her. 'I'm sorry, Mam. But I'm staying here. You'll have to see your own way home.'

Marlene stared in disbelief for a moment. Then she gathered her dignity together and stormed off into the night.

'Good riddance,' Mam said.

'Enough, Marjorie,' Eric warned.

Eunice looked absolutely appalled. 'I don't believe you lot! This is about us! It's about me and Helen! And look at you!'

'It's all right, Eunice,' Eric said. 'There'll be no more fighting.'

'Unbelievable,' Eunice hissed, shaking her head, and stomping off upstairs to our room. '*KOF KOF KOF.*'

I was left in the kitchen, alone, with the whole

mad scene ringing through my head. This is what lying and subterfuge had caused.

I should have known. I should have known no good would come of that giant shoe.

I was glad that we'd left it behind in our suite at the Hotel Grandissimo.

Chapter Seventeen

Eunice and I hadn't even thought about what it would be like at school on Monday.

It started as soon as we arrived.

We went in through the main gates, through the great mass of kids thronging about and gabbling about their weekends. We didn't speak to each other much, and that was quite normal. Eunice liked to pretend that we didn't belong together. We were approaching the main school buildings when the first voice rang out behind us.

'There she is! There's the Siamese girl off the telly!'

I looked round and it was a Year Six boy, pointing at us disbelievingly and trying to get everyone's attention.

'Look!' he cried, his voice breaking. 'It's her, isn't it?'

'Just ignore it,' Eunice said, walking closer beside me.

'Mary-Sue!' another voice yelled out. 'It's Mary-Sue off *Diva Wars!*'

Worse was to come as Eunice approached her friends: the lanky, skinny, trendy crowd from her year. They were popping gum and tutting and tossing their pony-tails as they waited for the bell to go.

They looked me and Eunice up and down, all scathingly, as if we were strangers.

'Go away,' hissed Eunice to me. 'Why are you following me around? My friends don't want you near them.'

Ah – this was the old Eunice talking! I shrugged.

'Go on, Helen.' She nudged me away with her elbow. 'They really can't stand you. They won't talk to me if you're with me. Go on! It's not like we're tied together any more.'

'Huh,' I said, and waited till a witty reply came into my head. But it didn't. I just moved away as Eunice skipped off to her tall, slim friends.

They still looked a bit sceptical about her.

'What's all this we've been hearing about *Diva Wars?*' one of the girls asked Eunice.

'What?' I heard my sister say. 'Nothing. Why?'

'It's just we heard that someone who looked like you was on that show on Saturday night. We can't stand that show. It wasn't you, was it, Eunice?

We might have a problem hanging around with someone as tacky as that . . .'

'No, of course not!' Eunice was squeaking. 'Why would I go on there? It's really tacky. *KOF KOF*. I wouldn't be on that show if they begged me!'

'That's okay, then,' said the leader of her bitchy gang. Then the whole lot of them, Eunice included, clip-clopped off in formation to go and bully some of the younger boys. Eunice didn't even spare me a backward glance. My sister's a coward, I thought. She'd say or do anything to keep in with those horrible friends of hers.

I was still thinking about this when I was in my tutor room and the register was being taken. I was off in a world of my own, swinging my legs on my too-high chair at my too-high desk right at the back of the classroom, which was where I preferred to be.

Then I realised Neil Fanshaw was leaning across to me and going, 'Pssst'. I pulled a face back at him because I don't appreciate being jolted out of a daydream. Then I felt bad because Neil's our tutor group's smelly kid and all the kids pick on him for it. He lives with just his dad, who's out working all the time, and I don't think it's all that clean round their house. 'What is it?' I asked him. And he passed me a badly-written note.

'It was you and your sister, wasn't it? On the telly. You were pretending! You're not Chinese!'

I sighed and crumpled up the note. I looked at him. 'It's Siamese,' I hissed.

He shrugged. 'Yeah, but you're not, are you?'

'What?'

'Joined up. Joined at the foot.'

I decided to brave it out. Neil was a bit thick. 'We are, actually. We've been joined together since birth.'

His eyes widened. 'So it really *was* you two on the telly? Are you going to win, do you think?' He looked really excited at the thought of sitting at the desk next to the next winner of *Diva Wars*. He didn't even think to ask how our Eunice could be in a separate part of the school to me, if we really were conjoined. Neil's dopey-looking face was so lit up with excitement I had to laugh.

'Don't be daft,' I told him. 'Of course it wasn't us! How could it have been?'

'Oh,' he said. 'Yeah, okay, right. It couldn't have been.'

Our form tutor, the formidable Ms Parsons, yelled at us then for talking at the back.

'I was just telling Neil that it wasn't me on *Diva Wars* on Saturday.'

'*Diva Wars!*' said our form tutor, with that weary

166

voice of hers. 'That's all you kids think about. Instant stardom. Instant gratification. You don't think you have to work for anything. You think it'll all just land in your lap.'

Our whole tutor group stared at Ms Parsons, as we often did when she went sounding off about the young people these days.

'But, Miss,' said Neil. 'It's true! If you win a show like that, you can become dead famous and rich overnight! That's dead good, isn't it?'

'You have to *struggle*,' said our form tutor. 'You have to *work* for things. Otherwise it's not worth it.'

Neil looked at her blankly. 'Why, Miss?'

Our tutor sat down heavily in her chair. It was first thing on Monday morning and she looked knackered already. 'God knows,' she said.

On the walk home from school, Eunice and I compared notes.

'Twenty-four times,' I said. 'Twenty-four different kids.'

'More like fifty for me,' she said. I knew she was exaggerating. She always had to come out on top.

'All of them thought it was us?' I asked.

She nodded.

We were hurrying home, on the quickest route there was, through the posh houses estate. We really didn't want anyone staring at us too long and hard, and we didn't want shouting at in the street.

'How did we think we could get away with it and not be noticed?' she said, close to tears.

'We just deny it, that's all,' I said. 'We just say we're lookalikes.'

'It's too obviously us,' Eunice said. 'The truth will come out *KOF* and we'll get into even more trouble, and look even stupider . . . *KOF KOF*.'

'Well, we're out of the show anyway now, aren't we? We just have to wait till the fuss dies down.'

But more fuss was waiting for us at home.

Mam and Eric had all of the newspapers out, spread open on the kitchen table. Mam was busy cutting out clippings and pasting them into a new scrapbook.

'Oh, hello, you two,' Eric said.

'Why've you bought all the papers?' I asked suspiciously. They had every single newspaper I'd ever seen. Even the nastier tabloids and the hugest of the big papers. Even before Mam said anything, I knew what was behind this. 'We're in them, aren't we?' I slung my school bag in the corner, where it would stay till the next morning, homework not done.

'In the papers?' Eunice squealed.

Mam nodded. 'There are some beautiful pictures

of you! There's even pictures of me and Eric! Looking all proud and doting.'

I sat down crossly while Eunice went rummaging through the pages of clippings.

We were going to be made famous! There seemed to be absolutely no escape whatsoever from this fiasco.

'Cheer up, princess,' Eric grinned, seeing my face. 'You'll never guess what all the papers are saying?'

'That we're complete fakes? That we should be put in prison for fraud?'

He laughed. 'Not at all.'

Eunice and Mam, rustling all the newspapers, threatened to drown out mine and Eric's conversation. 'What are they saying then?' I asked him. 'Tell me, then!'

He laughed. 'They're saying you two are brilliant! They are saying that Mary-Sue is the popstar sensation of the season!'

'Oh my god,' I said quietly.

'And,' Mam jumped up, waving her scissors about excitedly, 'word has got out that you've been chucked out of the competition! There's been a leak to the press! And they've all gone crackers about it!'

Eric patted my shoulder. 'They're all saying you

should be given another chance. They're saying it's a scandal and that you should go back on there.'

'Back . . .' I said. 'Back onto the show?'

Mam, Eric and Eunice were all looking at me.

'They think we're marvellous,' Eunice said, looking up from what she'd been reading. 'They think we're the best thing *ever!*'

Chapter Eighteen

What happened next was Agatha Staynes.

I was trogging downstairs in my nightie, my eyes all bleary with sleep. It was just after eight the next morning and Mam started screaming in the living room.

All three of them were in there, pointing at the telly and yelling at each other.

'What is it?' I said, wishing they would quieten down.

'Agatha!' Eunice burst out. 'She's *On the Settee with Fenula Before Nine!*' That show was one of Eunice's favourites. She liked to catch it before leaving for school: it was all make-up, dieting tips, and celebrity gossip.

On the screen there was a celebrity we knew very well. 'What's she saying?' I drew nearer.

Agatha was in one of her pinky-purple feathery-floaty outfits. She was even more caring and serious than ever this morning. She was facing the camera and looking out at the world with a woeful expression.

'Has someone died?' I asked.

'Sssssshhh!' said Mam, waving for silence.

'. . . it's amazing to think, in this hi-tech world, where everything is bang-up-to-the-minute and any kind of information is only the touch of a button away, that we could lose track of people like this. It seems just about impossible that anyone could fall down the cracks in society and be lost from view for ever.'

'Indeed,' said Scottish Fenula, who was sitting across from Agatha, on a settee of her own. 'And you say that the reason Mary-Sue and her family have vanished from sight is that they gave the producers of *Diva Wars* false names?'

We all looked at Mam.

'I had to!' she hissed. 'So they wouldn't find out you were fake Siamese twins!'

'That's right,' said Agatha on the telly. 'For some reason that poor family felt the need to adopt a fake identity for our show. And now, when we need to, we have absolutely no way of being able to get in touch with them.'

'Well, that's just awful,' said Fenula. 'So you're putting out a special plea, aren't you, Agatha? For the relatives or friends of Mary-Sue to step forward and let us know where they are and where they live?'

'That's right, Fenula,' Agatha said. 'We simply *have* to find them.'

Eunice grabbed my arm and made a strange squeaking noise.

'As viewers will see in this coming Saturday's episode of *Diva Wars*, Mary-Sue has been rejected from the second round by my colleague, Trevor Rotter. This might come as a shock to the viewing millions who believe like me, that, Mary-Sue is by far the most talented and exciting performer in our competition . . .'

Mam started whooping with triumph and Eric joined in. We couldn't hear the next few words.

'. . . so that's why I'm starting a campaign. I'm taking it upon myself to have this silly decision to remove Mary-Sue revoked. I will make that Trevor Rotter eat his words. But first – we have to find Mary-Sue and her family! And that's why I'm on your show, Fenula. This is the biggest and most-watched morning show and I knew you would really care about the fate of those poor, talented, conjoined twins . . .' Agatha looked very doleful and worried. She was doing a real star turn.

'Indeed,' said Fenula. 'I saw last Saturday's show, just like everyone else, and I was completely blown away by their phenomenal performance. That three-legged dancing! And they're so bonny, aren't they? I thought they were real stars in the making. I can't believe Trevor Rotter had them chucked out . . .'

'I can,' said Agatha. 'The man is evil. And he wants that soppy Evelina Semolina to win.'

A number was at the bottom of the screen. 'Do you know the whereabouts of the singing Siamese twins? Then phone now!'

Mam shot over to the phone. 'I'm ringing in!' she said.

'Hang on, hang on,' said Eric. 'Are we quite sure about this?'

Mam looked blank, the receiver up to her ear and all ready to jab the numbers in. 'What do you mean?'

'You haven't asked the girls yet. You don't know whether they want to return to that madhouse. They might not want to start pretending again. Especially after what my mam said and everything . . .'

'Psshaw.' Mam waved his objections away. 'They won't be swayed by her qualms. Of course they wouldn't! You still want to be a star, don't you, girls? You'd want to go back to *Diva Wars* if you could, wouldn't you?'

Mam looked at us so beseechingly it was hard not to refuse her. We just stood there, though, staring at her.

'Well?' Mam gasped out. 'Shall I phone or not?'

I could sense Eunice, all immaculate in her school uniform, trembling beside me in excitement. I knew that she was about to burst any second. Of course she wanted to return to the contest. I knew she was about to give in. So I spoke up.

'We can't,' I said.

Mam frowned. 'How come? And don't say you don't believe in cheating. Everyone cheats! Don't listen to Marlene. She never made it anywhere!'

Eric frowned at Mam's harshness. But Mam's attention was riveted on me.

'We can't do it because of one very practical reason,' I said.

'Whaaaat?' Mam was getting impatient.

'We left something behind at the Hotel Grandissimo,' I said.

Weirdly enough, Agatha Staynes had chosen that precise moment to show the cameras and Fenula and the people at home the object that she had brought into the studio in a large pink box. I had been watching the screen out of the corner of my eye, and I gasped at the coincidence when Agatha opened the box.

'There,' I said. 'That's what we left behind.'

Agatha was unravelling protective tissue paper and revealing for the cameras our sparkling and oversized dancing shoe.

'They left this in their suite at the Hotel Grandissimo,' Agatha told Fenula. 'I can't help seeing it as a sign that they think their performing days are over.' She held the gorgeous scarlet shoe up for the clearest view. 'I want to persuade them to wear it once more,' said Agatha Staynes determinedly. 'And I want to persuade the producers of the show that, if we can find the Siamese twins who fit this giant dancing shoe, then they should be returned to the *Diva Wars* – immediately!'

Chapter Nineteen

I dug my feet in.

'No,' I said. 'I want to think about it first.'

Mam was all for phoning the hotline immediately. 'We have to get in there! While they're all keen! If they let you back in, you'll be bound to win. You'll have public opinion on your side!'

I was determined, though. I didn't want to rush back into it.

'Let the girl decide for herself, Marjorie,' Eric urged.

Mam flashed him a dangerous look. 'Eunice wants to go back, don't you, love? You'd be back there like a shot, wouldn't you?'

Eunice nodded nervously.

'Let me think about it,' I said.

'What's to think about?' Mam shouted.

She wanted it so badly. And I had to decide: if I did this, would it be for our sake, or for Mam's?

*

Days passed, and me and Eunice went to school.

'Are you them? Are you the Siamese sisters?'

'Go on! Tell us!'

'Do we look like Siamese twins? *KOF!*' Eunice would holler.

'No, but you look like *them*! Are you *fake* Siamese twins, then?'

Eunice and I would look at each other and think: people are getting too close to the truth. And, at those moments, we wanted to keep our heads down and away from the public eye.

Days passed and Agatha Staynes stepped up her campaign to publicise the search for Mary-Sue. She went on chat shows and talk shows, kids' TV shows and even the news. Mam sat home, glued to the TV while we were at school, video-taping every appearance Agatha made. She played them to us in the evenings, like she was brainwashing us.

'You're breaking that poor old woman's heart!' Mam cried.

We saw Trevor Rotter on the *Seven O'Clock News*. 'Even if Mary-Sue re-emerges from obscurity and begs us to be back on *Diva Wars*, it will be over my dead body!'

'Worm!' Mam yelled at the telly. 'Scumbag! Drongo!'

Days passed and Eric brought home all the

newspapers and all the magazines that carried the story. We were on the cover of three TV guides and five of the gossip magazines! We sat there stunned, as Eric skilfully scissored out our pictures and stuck them into our nicely full scrapbook.

'You look very nice on the cover of *Hiya!* magazine,' he told me.

I blushed and had a look. He was right, though. It was a shot of me and Eunice practising our dancing in the ballroom at the Hotel Grandissimo. I looked all animated and punky, and really into my dancing, grinning away like crazy. Weirdly, Eunice didn't look as nice as me. She looked a bit sweaty and like she was counting steps in her head. She was pulling a funny face. 'Let me see that!' she gasped. 'I look awful! I look bloody terrible! *KOFKOFKOF!!*' Then, before we could stop her, she had ripped the cover of *Hiya!* magazine into little shreds.

'You selfish little madam!' Eric shouted, appalled by her. 'Just because your sister looked nicer than you did – in one measly photo! That was rotten, Eunice. Get to your room!'

Eunice's eyes widened in astonishment. 'You what?' she said, starting to laugh. 'You're telling me what to do? You? Who the hell are you? My mam's fat new fancy man? *KOF! KOF!* And you're telling *me* off? Pah!'

Eunice got up then and stormed out of the house, slamming the kitchen door behind her.

'Ooops,' Eric said. 'I shouldn't have told her off. Marjorie won't like that.'

'She deserved a good slap,' I said, staring miserably at the ripped bits of my magazine cover. 'She's getting way above herself lately.'

'Too big for her giant shoe,' Eric said, and we both laughed.

'Don't listen to what she says,' I told him. 'Like, when she said you were fat and Mam's fancy man and stuff.'

He shrugged and started tidying up all our press clippings. That's what he had called them – press clippings! Like we really *were* famous and all. 'I am, though, aren't I? That's all I am. A fat fancy man.'

'Don't worry about Eunice,' I said. 'She doesn't have respect for anyone. And she's only nice to me lately because she needs me to be Mary-Sue with her.'

'Tell you what,' Eric said. 'Let's go out and get you another copy of *Hiya!*'

We had to get some groceries, anyway. Mam was upstairs with one of her bad heads. She was also digging through her old tapes and CDs, sounding out likely songs we might use, should we decide to return to the *Diva Wars*.

180

'She won't give up, will she?' I asked Eric, as we rumbled along in his clunky old car, heading towards the big supermarket. 'She'll keep on at us, persuading us.'

'It's not fair, really,' he said. 'She should let you choose.' It was a surprise, to hear him come this close to criticising Mam.

'If we don't do it, what will she say?' I wondered aloud, watching all the houses and bus stops flick by. 'She'll never forgive me, will she?'

Eric didn't say anything.

In the supermarket he even let me push the trolley, which is something I don't normally get to do, being too little. Eric went dashing all over the aisles, picking stuff up and consulting the list he had made. He was buying things we never bought – carpet cleaner and furniture polish and stuff. He was more of a home-maker than Mam ever was. He brought me a replacement issue of *Hiya!*, too, and I stared at the cover as we ambled along, up and down the aisles. It was true – I looked fantastic in that photo. Me! Dwarfish, squished-looking me, on the cover of a gossipy celebrity magazine!

When we were loading things onto the conveyor belt, I was in a proper trance.

'It's you, isn't it?' It was a big coffee-coloured

woman with dyed blonde hair, ringing our groceries up on her till. She grinned at me and Eric. 'It is her, isn't it? Her on all the magazines?'

We both opened our mouths to speak, but then the woman's face fell. 'But where's your sister? Aren't you and she meant to be fixed together?' She frowned heavily. 'Hey, what's going on here? Don't you know the whole world's out looking for you?'

Eric did some lightning-quick thinking. 'We've been in Switzerland.'

'Switzerland?' The woman had stopped ringing up our purchases. It was as if she wouldn't let us through until she had been given a satisfactory explanation. 'What's in Switzerland?'

'A very expensive clinic,' Eric said. 'The girls have been surgically separated.'

'WHAAT??' cried the lady behind the till. 'And didn't you know they was looking for you? All the TV people and that Staynes woman?'

We shook our heads. 'How could we know? We were out of the contest and out of the country, getting surgically separated.'

The woman shook her head disbelievingly. 'Then you'd better get yourselves back together! You'd better get yourselves back on the TV!' She squinted hard at me. 'It is you, in't it? It really is you?'

I nodded proudly, but Eric urged me quickly

through the till. Other shoppers were beginning to notice us. The big woman was standing up and yelling to her friend who worked at the basket-only till. 'Jamila, look at this! It's one of them girls! Only she's been and gone to Switzerland and have her sister chopped off her foot! And them two being so overnight-famous like they are!'

'What's that, Precious?' cried Jamila. 'You've seen them Siamese twins?'

'Right here!' our till lady bawled. 'Standing right here without her sister!'

We watched all eyes turn towards us. Suddenly there was a crowd surging down the frozen-food aisle and the biscuit aisle, alerted by all the shouting. They were pushing and shoving and trying to get a glimpse of me. Eric decided we had to abandon our shopping where it was. He picked me up and slung me over his shoulder and we ran for it! Straight out of the supermarket and out to the car.

'Stop him!' Precious bellowed. 'He's stealing one of them Siamese twins!'

At home Mam was cross about the abandoned shopping, but she was thrilled to hear about all the kerfuffle and the crowd that had gathered around us. She was very intrigued, also, by the story Eric had spun them and invented on the spot.

'Maybe people would believe it,' she mused. 'That we went to a special hospital, all secretly, and had the girls separated . . .'

'But we have to work as a team!' Eunice – who had returned in our absence – protested. 'We need to be a single entity! Because she sings brilliantly and I look fabulous!'

I turned to stare at our Eunice. That was a compliment she'd just given me! Amazing!

Eric was shaking his head. 'A secret operation! What was I thinking of?' He looked thoroughly ashamed of himself. 'This is getting sicker and sicker. I wish we'd never even started this terrible business . . .'

Mam laughed. 'But it was your idea, you idiot! All this Siamese stuff is down to you and your sick mind!'

'We've dug ourselves in too deep,' he said. 'We've made the children lie on national TV. We've started something we can't even finish . . .'

Mam emptied her glass. 'We would never have done it, if you hadn't come up with the idea.'

Eric lashed out angrily. 'Were you happy with failing all the time, Marjorie? Were you happy coming back empty-handed from every audition? Were you?'

'Of c-course not . . .'

'Well, then. That's why you were quick to jump on my idea. Because you could see that we'd be successful. And now – in a way – we are.'

'We have to go through with it,' Mam said fiercely. 'We have to return to the show.'

She was looking at Eunice and me.

After our experience at the supermarket, I now knew that there was no going back.

We had a showbiz destiny, Eunice and me – as Mary-Sue. And we had to meet that destiny.

We had a public to face.

Chapter Twenty

We watched Saturday's show together, and the occasion was more strained and less celebratory than the previous week's. This was the show all about Round Two in the Hotel Grandissimo.

'Just look at her!' Trevor Rotter was saying. 'Isn't she wonderful? She can do anything! I bet she's going to be our winner, at the end of *Diva Wars!*'

He was talking about Evelina Semolina, who was simpering at the camera in her dayglo lime-green leotard. All our family booed at the screen. Evelina's mother was standing very close beside the gargantuan Rotter.

'I hope my daughter, Evelina, will win,' Mrs Semolina was saying. 'She certainly deserves to. She's perfect in every respect. There's nothing wrong with *her!*'

They were grinning in a sickly kind of way, and then the show returned to the studio, where an audience was applauding wildly and the judges were sitting together and grimacing at each other.

Agatha Staynes looked flushed and all het up. It had been a very busy week of campaigning for her. She had been on every TV show she could get her face on, talked to every journalist and called in every favour. But still she hadn't managed to find Mary-Sue.

We hadn't phoned in yet. I had put Mam off. I wanted to watch this show first and then see what I thought. I was glad, too, that none of those women from the supermarket had phoned in to report us. If anyone was going to phone in, it was going to be one of our family!

On the telly, Trevor was baiting Agatha.

'So, even after all your feeble attempts this week to bring your dancing Siamese twins to light, you've still failed, Agatha.'

'Not yet, I haven't,' she warned him. 'I'm not giving up!'

'Even if you find Mary-Sue,' he said, 'and get them to wear that big shoe again, they won't be allowed back into the contest. They have been chucked out fair and square . . .'

The studio audience booed him! There was a huge rumble of discontent from the banks of seats, and for a moment Trevor looked disconcerted.

'It wasn't fair and square!' Wanda Needlebottom broke in. 'You chucked them out when me and Agatha were nowhere near! There was no vote, no consensus. You just got rid of them because you didn't like them!'

The audience grew even louder in their protest at this.

'It was sheer prejudice!' Agatha cried. 'He didn't like those conjoined girls the first time he set eyes on them, and he said as much, too. He said they were *weird*.'

'Well, they *are* weird,' he shrugged, and the audience cried out in dismay and anger.

Trevor suddenly saw that public opinion was going against him.

'When we find them, we have to let them join in again!' Wanda cried, and got a big round of applause.

'No no no!' Trevor yelled. 'Evelina Semolina! That's who the audience want to see! A perfect little girl with absolutely nothing wrong with her ...' Huge boos at this.

At home, Eunice gasped. 'They're booing Evelina's name! They hate her now!'

'It's you two they love,' Mam said.

'It's a disgrace!' Agatha said. 'This is all about Trevor's prejudice about people who look a bit different. He's been like this every year. But we won't let him get his own way, will we, everyone?'

A huge cry of 'Nooo!' went up from the crowd.

And then Agatha announced a new phase in her protest against Trevor.

'I want to invite onto the stage three very special people who have come here tonight, to add their voices to mine, to ask Mary-Sue, wherever she is, to pick up the phone and come back to us . . .'

Really soppy, sentimental music started up and Agatha threw up her hands in welcome.

'Here they come! Three of the most special and differently-abled superstars we've discovered in recent years!'

'Oh, crikey,' Eric whispered. 'What have we started?'

Agatha was joined on stage by three small figures and she announced them one at a time. I realised that the music was some old Whitney Houston number – 'The Greatest Love of All' – and all three of the very special guest stars were singing it along with Agatha. Dry-ice smoke wreathed around them dramatically as the spotlights picked them out. Agatha had taken over the whole show!

'Here they are, ladies and gentlemen! Three of the bravest stars in the showbiz firmament . . . come to protest at the unfair dismissal of our Siamese celebrities! Here's – Loulabelle Radcliffe! Winner of *Search for a Celeb!*'

Huge applause for Loulabelle, the girl with one single eye, smack-dab in the middle of her forehead.

'And here's Tony Tomorrow from *Talent Parade!*'

Big roar of approval for Tony, who had a huge head and no nose.

'And finally, from *Star Turn* . . . it's Belladonna Arkwright!'

She was the oddest-looking one of the whole bunch. She had no eyebrows.

'Sing everyone! Sing out loud!' Agatha cried out, weeping now. The three children's voices were like an angelic choir. 'Sing out and call out to Mary-Sue! Make her see that learning to love yourself is the greatest love of all! And that being conjoined shouldn't be any set-back to winning a competition like *Diva Wars!*'

The audience were joining in and singing along. They swayed and raised their arms in the air. Some of them had banners with huge glittering shoes painted on.

'Sing out, everyone,' carolled Agatha Staynes, 'and let them know that they are loved!'

The show finished shortly after that.

At home, we all kept very quiet.

'The world's gone completely crazy,' Eric said quietly.

Then our phone rang. Mam snatched it up. 'Yes? Hello?' She frowned heavily. 'Oh, it's you. What do you want? Have you phoned to chew off my ear some more?'

We looked at Eric. 'Is it my mam?' he said. Our mam nodded. She was listening intently to Marlene at the other end.

'What's she saying?' Eric said, standing up. I knew that he felt guilty about his mam. He hadn't been in touch with her since her row with our mam a full week ago.

'I see,' Mam was saying, thoughtfully, chewing on the lemon slice out of her glass. 'Right. Okay. That's fine. Good.' She nodded. 'Okay, Marlene. We'll see you then.' Mam put the phone down. 'That was your mother,' she told Eric.

'I know! What did she say?'

'The producers of *Diva Wars* contacted her . . .'

Eric looked shocked. 'How? How did they track us down through her?'

Mam shook her head. 'It wasn't that. They wanted her to go on, of her own account. Being a dwarf and winning *Starry Eyes* in 1974. They wanted her to join the campaign to get Mary-Sue back in the contest.'

'Oh,' said Eric. He was imagining what his mam would have said to the producers. She'd have blasted them!

'She's changed her mind,' Mam said. 'She didn't say anything awful to them. And she didn't tell the truth!'

'*KOF! What? KOF!*' said Eunice.

'What did she tell them?' I asked.

'She told them where we live,' Mam said. 'She said, "Yes! I know the twins! I know where they live! And I agree! I happen to agree with Agatha Staynes! They certainly deserve to win *Diva Wars* and become the biggest conjoined stars in the world!"'

Chapter Twenty-One

Down in Broad Bottom, Eric's mam was delighted to see us again. She hugged Eunice and me very fiercely outside The Dirty Duck.

'Now look, girls – I still don't approve of cheating and conniving ... but I do realise how much you both want to get to the top of the showbiz tree, and I can't blame you for trying every which way you can, to climb those showbiz branches.' Marlene looked up at our mam, and the two women exchanged polite but wary greetings. 'I was wrong, I suppose, to attack you, Marjorie,' Marlene conceded. 'I realise that you were only doing your best for your girls.'

'I was,' Mam said. 'I'll always do my best for them.'

'You were right, too,' Marlene said ruefully. 'Perhaps if I had lied and connived and cheated a bit more, I'd have been a bigger star than I ever was. You have to be hard as nails to get on in this game.

Or have someone behind you who can be hard when it's required.'

Mam nodded. 'It's true. I'd do anything to see my daughters become stars.'

Marlene nodded, and waved us inside The Dirty Duck. 'I've got a surprise for you two,' she said. And, in the saloon bar, she introduced us to Fred the cobbler from the village, who had made our first three special shoes. Now Marlene had commissioned a new set from him: dancing shoes in midnight-blue patent leather. Two regular size, one extra-large.

'They're beautiful!' we gasped in unison.

'Just you see that they take you dancing all the way to the top!' Marlene said. She went to fetch some drinks for everyone.

'Thanks, Mam,' Eric said to her.

She shrugged. 'You lot belong with each other, Eric. I've watched you, and the four of you are a proper little family.'

'I know,' he said. He cleared his throat and looked awkward. He glanced at Mam and she nodded quickly. 'That's why ... I've ... um ... I've ...'

We all stared at him. I think I knew what was coming next.

'Come on, man!' Marlene laughed. 'Spit it out!'

Eric stammered some more, and Mam burst out: 'We're getting married! At Christmas! He only just asked me last night.'

Eunice and I stared at them dumbfounded. We knew it was serious – but, marriage! Mam had often said she'd never be daft enough to shackle herself to anyone.

Never get into anything you can't wriggle out of – that was her motto.

She liked to be free. She liked to be on the move. That's why we'd changed homes so often, and why we had been in and out of different schools. All of those things were symptoms of what Mam called her 'restless needs'.

I reminded her of those, when we all toasted the marriage in fizzy orange.

'I reckon it's time I tied myself down a bit more,' she told me. 'And don't you like Eric? Don't you think he's all right?'

I nodded, smiling. 'I think he's great, Mam.'

I had done ever since that very first Sunday, back at the car-boot sale in Denton.

When we phoned Agatha Staynes, she screamed down the phone.

I've never heard anyone quite so excited as that. Eunice and I had the receiver between us; we were both talking to her, and she took a good three minutes to calm down again.

'Did you see the show last night? Did you girls watch *Diva Wars*? Have you seen how much campaigning I've done on your behalf? What did you think, eh? It's all for you! Because I think you're marvellous and you deserve to win. Did you think it went too far? Maybe it was a bit schmaltzy and tacky, bringing Loulabelle and Tony and Belladonna on the stage ... but ... but everyone wanted to protest against the injustice! Everyone thought it was a complete disgrace that you were thrown off the show!'

I was beginning to think that we would never get a word in edgeways.

'And what a coincidence!' Agatha gabbled on. 'That we contacted Marlene to help with our protest about the differently-abled, and it turns out she's going to be your new grandmother!'

'I know,' I said, 'it's amazing. And I hear that she's going to sing a special song on the show next Saturday?'

'That's right,' said Agatha. 'It was her idea to come on, as an oppressed and differently-abled superstar from the past. She thought it would be nice to sing once more for her public, and we agreed with her.'

Much as I adored Marlene I did wonder if the offer of being on telly had changed her mind about our 'lying and conniving'.

'You're going to come on the show and rejoin the contest, aren't you, girls?' Agatha asked. 'You're going to come to the studios in Manchesterford and rejoin the *Diva Wars* for the live quarter-final?'

I knew by the way her voice was going all dramatic, that she was being filmed at the other end. Already we were back in the story!

'Yes,' we told her, speaking as one. 'Mary-Sue is coming back!'

Saturday! And it felt like we were getting a hero's welcome wherever we went!

On the train we were told we'd been upgraded to first class, and so we were led along to special seats right at the front of the train. Word had gone round that we were returning to the show, and people were pointing at us. They nudged each other and waved at us. We were brought free drinks and snacks on the train, and people watched to see if we ate with both mouths. To look convincing, we'd rehearsed this act where I would take a swig of pop and Eunice would go, 'Delicious!' And she would take a bite of her baguette and I would say, 'Scrumptious!'

Mam, Eric and Marlene were of course travelling with us, and they were all togged up in their newest outfits. All five of us were gobsmacked with excitement. Mam was proud and quiet: she had taken a bunch of tranquilliser pills before setting off, to ensure that she wouldn't flare up at all. Marlene couldn't stop herself gabbling and prattling away. She was returning to the bright lights of showbiz! After all these years! She had packed six of her favourite gowns, and couldn't settle on which she wanted to wear for her number. Her number was 'I Am What I Am' and she was kicking off the live quarter-final show. 'I'm not sure I can still do it!' she said, looking stricken. 'Maybe I don't have the old magic any more.'

'Of course you do,' Eric told her gently.

Out of all of us, only Eric was managing to keep his head. We were glad he was in charge, looking after the mundane but necessary things, such as our tickets and luggage.

'Going back to showbiz is like going back into battle!' Marlene said. Her mind was obviously whizzing with new showbiz similes. 'Making a comeback is like making a pie! Or going on a quest! Or running a marathon!'

Eunice and I kept exchanging glances. This was really happening! We really were going back to become stars! We swung our feet together, to the rhythm of the train.

By afternoon we arrived in the echoingly cavernous station in the heart of the city of Manchesterford.

'This is it, girls,' Eric said. 'Now, just you keep your cool, remember.'

His mam looked like she was going to faint with pleasure, when she saw our reception committee.

We were welcomed on our platform by a brass band and flashing cameras. Agatha Staynes herself was there, in a flowing, sequinned kaftan. She flung open her arms to us.

'Oh, my dears! My dears! My poor conjoined megastars! Welcome, welcome back to the *Diva Wars!*'

All of this was being filmed. I felt dozens of lenses on us, moving in for the close-ups, as Eunice and I were gathered up into Agatha's bosom.

'I have found you! I found you! I brought you back!'

Then we formed a kind of procession through the station, with the crowds drawing apart to let us through. Everyone watched us peg-legging along and applauded our bravery. Eunice whispered into my ear, 'It's all a bit tacky, isn't it?' And I nodded, knowing that neither of us cared how tacky it was.

This was our moment! And we were completely sure that we were going to win!

Chapter Twenty-Two

The car that took us to our hotel had the radio playing, and Evelina Semolina was being interviewed. She was shrill with outrage at the news we were back in town.

'Of course I don't think that they – she – *it* – ought to be allowed back into the contest. My mummy and my lawyer think it's extremely unfair and probably actionable. If Mary-Sue wins *Diva Wars* then I will have been robbed. Besides, who wants to look at *freaks* on the television? They aren't at all talented. And it's only the short, ugly one who does any actual singing. People just feel sorry for them ...' Our driver clicked the radio off and put a stop to her whining.

We drove through the heart of the city, with these tall impressive buildings rising up all silvery around us. I think we were all dazzled. Even more dazzled by our hotel, which was even grander than the Hotel Grandissimo. This time we were staying in the Hotel Magnifico! And again we had a suite at the very top.

In the foyer, Agatha bid us a hasty goodbye. 'We must part here, my dears. I have to return to the studios and make sure that everything is prepared for tonight's show. And you must prepare yourselves too, and be ready to knock everyone's socks off!' She grinned and then swirled away in her shimmering kaftan.

'Well!' Marlene chuckled. 'She's just the same in real life, isn't she?'

I noticed that Mam was starting to look nervous. Her tranquillisers were starting to wear off.

'Let's go and see this suite!' Eric said heartily, calling over a porter.

'So much could go wrong!' Mam said. 'So much can still go wrong!'

Eric shook his head. 'Not now,' he said. 'This, my love, is where the high life begins. You just see.'

The suite was fabulous. Much more fabulous than the one we had been given in Brumlington-on-Sea. But the opulent charms of our suite were nothing compared with our next little surprise.

The five of us were just standing at the huge picture window in our suite, gazing out at the roof-tops of Manchesterford and into the far distance, when we saw a helicopter come whizzing down out of the sky and land on the rooftop beside us.

Mam screamed.

Eric was laughing.

She turned to him. 'You knew that was going to happen!'

He nodded. 'Agatha planned it. It's our transport to the studios!'

Mam was choked up and just about crying. 'It's . . . what I've always wanted!'

'I know,' he said, pulling open the French windows.

There was a terrace at the top of the hotel, far above the city. Our helicopter had touched down on a special landing pad, right by our suite. We dashed out to see it and it was a perfect, silver monster. The pilot waved at us and told us we had better gather everything we needed. There was just time to take a spin across the city and get us to the studios.

'This is true glamour,' Mam said, sighing. 'This is everything I've ever dreamed of.'

She sounded so calm and relaxed in the back of the helicopter. I don't think the rest of us were. We were weaving and diving between tall buildings, and then being hurled upwards into the endless blue of the sky. The noise was terrific and I felt like I had to keep swallowing hard, to prevent all my internal organs jumping out of my mouth. Eunice gripped one of my hands, digging her nails in out of fear, rather than malice. Marlene was holding my other hand, repeating some mantra under her breath. I thought she was praying at first, then I realised she was running through the words of her song.

'Isn't this what I told you we'd do, some day, girls?' Mam turned to us and grinned. 'We're in a helicopter! We're not tied to anything! This is complete freedom!'

We tried to smile and look pleased, but I think we were both too terrified. How come Mam didn't mind heights?

'I don't care now,' Mam went on, 'whether we win or not. I don't really mind what happens. So long as you two do your best. So long as you just enjoy it. That's all that's important. I've had my dream. This is my ambition! Doing this! Zipping about in the sky like this!' She looked at Eric and tousled his thinning hair. 'And I'm going to marry this man, who's turned out to be the man of my dreams.'

We watched them kissing, and it wasn't even that disgusting!

Mam sat straight in her seat. 'Actually, I feel a bit sick,' she said.

'WE'RE HERE!' Marlene shrieked, above the whipping noise of the wind and the drone of the rotors. And, sure enough, we were homing in on the famous Manchesterford Studios. Far, far below, crowds were thronging. Coaches were arriving, crammed with audience members; limousines were pulling up and letting out celebrities. Red carpets were being unrolled, spotlights were springing brilliantly to life.

There was a landing pad on top of the building and we were dropping gracefully into place: making the most dramatic entrance of them all . . .

Chapter Twenty-Three

We were whisked through the building to the star dressing rooms. Corridors and faces passed in a blur and I just knew that everyone wanted to get a look at us. An excited hubbub followed us around as we descended the levels, down through the studios and into the basement. Agatha Staynes led the way, warning everyone to stand well back: the infamous Siamese twins were coming through!

I was going through the words of our song. We hadn't rehearsed as much as I'd have liked to. But it was a song we both knew really well, an old Eurythmics number, 'Sisters Are Doing It For Themselves'. It was Eric's suggestion.

'This one,' said Agatha at last, wheezing, as she shoved open a certain dressing-room door. Someone had hastily pinned up two golden stars with our name on. 'It's the roomiest and nicest dressing room we have,' she said. 'And it was supposed to be Evelina Semolina's! But now you're back, we've had her chucked out!' Agatha looked delighted that Evelina had been ousted. She had no time for that simpering idiot, either.

We hurried in and sighed. Flowers! Chocolates! and – BANG!! Mam opened the champagne almost before we were through the door.

'This is really going to make Evelina furious,' Eunice laughed. 'I hope she doesn't try any kind of – *KOF* – sabotage . . . *KOF KOF*.' I tried thumping her on the back. 'I'll be *KOF* okay.'

'Have some champagne,' Mam said, passing round paper cups.

'Probably not a good idea,' Marlene frowned. She was just about invisible under the bags containing her six favourite gowns. 'Now, Agatha. Perhaps you could point me in the direction of *my* dressing room?'

'Oh yes.' Agatha glugged back her champagne and stirred into life. 'They've given you the same one you had for the 1974 final of *Starry Eyes*! Just for good luck!'

'Oooh, marvellous!' said Marlene, with very starry eyes indeed. She was just about to be led off, to prepare herself for her number. She turned to us first. 'I want to wish you girls the very best of luck,' she said. 'Whatever happens this evening, I think you're all stars. And I'm glad that you are all a family now. I'm so glad to be part of that family.'

We all hugged Marlene – even Mam – and then she scurried off down the corridor to her own dressing room.

Eunice was still coughing. 'I hope I can stop,' she said, looking worried all of a sudden. 'I can't go out there – *KOF KOF!* – coughing like mad!'

Mam was checking out all the make-up and peering at herself in the lavish mirrors. 'Oh, it'll be okay. Don't think about it. Calm down!'

A voice came crackling over the tannoy, warning us we only had twenty minutes till we had to go on air. Eunice gave a sharp scream and started coughing even harder.

'Where did the time go?' Eric said, wonderingly.

'It's all the excitement,' Mam sighed. 'Have you noticed? When your life is boring and rubbish, and nothing ever happens to you, time just takes ages to go by. But when the good stuff eventually rolls along it goes: WHHOOOOSSSHH!'

Eric topped up their champagne. 'WHHOOO-SSHH! You're right!'

'*KOF KOF KOF KOF KOF!*' went Eunice.

'Let's make our lives good enough to go WHHOOOSSSHH all the time,' Mam said.

'We will,' promised Eric.

'Err,' I said. 'I think our Eunice is choking . . .'

'I'm not,' she said. '*KOF KOF*, I'm all *KOF* right *KOFKOFFFKOF*.'

Just then the dressing-room door swung open. We all looked to see who would come in like that, without knocking. My heart skipped a beat! There, in full, devastating make-up, stood our arch nemesis and rival diva, Evelina Semolina! She was slathered in glitter and jewellery and everything about her was expensive and gorgeous. Her frock just about screamed 'Triumphant Queen Diva of the Whole Galaxy!' at us.

'What do you want?' I growled at her.

'Why,' she simpered. 'That's not a very friendly greeting. Not to the girl who gave up her dressing room for you!'

'You called us freaks on the radio!' I shouted. I felt like dashing over there and smacking her one. I could ruffle her feathers a bit. But I was attached to Eunice, who was going convulsive with all her coughing. '*KOFKOFKOFKOFFITYKOFKOF-KOF!*'

'What's wrong with her?' Evelina said.

'She always coughs when she's nervous,' I said.

'Nervous, eh?' Evelina laughed. She threw open the dressing-room fridge. 'Here. She should drink something. This will do the trick.' She produced a bottle of something sickly-looking and pink.

'What's that?'

Evelina unscrewed the bottle's top and smelled the contents dreamily. 'It's a fab new drink that I'm sponsoring. It's called Scrumptious Semolina Fizz.'

'That sounds disgusting!' I took the bottle and saw that there was a picture of Evelina's face on it!

'*KOFKOFKOF*,' went our Eunice. She grabbed the bottle off me. 'I'll drink *KOFKOF* anything right *KOF* now,' she gasped.

'Toodle-oo!' Evelina Semolina twittered, taking her leave. 'We may have had our differences in the past and, even if I do believe that it's a gross unfairness that you've been allowed to take part, I do wish you the very best of luck with tonight's performance!'

She closed the dressing-room door behind her.

'Maybe she's not so bad after all,' Mam said, blearily finishing the champagne.

'Huh,' said Eric. 'She's an idiot! She's a sickly-sweet simpering fool!'

Eunice was glugging back the Semolina Fizz. I couldn't think of a more disgusting drink! Fizzy semolina!

Eunice stopped and put down the bottle. We all looked at her.

'Hmm.' She frowned. 'I think I've stopped coughing.'

We waited.

'Thank goodness for that,' Eric said.

'That didn't taste too bad, either,' said Eunice.

'Right,' I said. 'We haven't got time for any more messing about. We have to get into costume straight away and—'

Mam gave a little scream.

'Marjorie, what is it?'

'Our Eunice! She's gone a funny colour!'

Eunice was looking a bit florid. 'What?' she gasped. 'What do you mean?' She looked like she was blushing all over.

'It's that drink!' Eric cried. 'There was something in that drink!'

'Oh, I don't think so,' Eunice said, sitting back on the sofa. 'I mean, if there was, then I'd ZZZZ-ZZZZzzzzzzzzz.'

We froze.

Eunice had dropped into the deepest sleep EVER.

'EUNICE!' Mam dashed over to us and started shaking her hard. 'WAKE UP!'

'ZZZZZZZZZzzzzzZZZZZZzzzzzzzzzzzZZZZZZZ,' went Eunice.

'Oh crikey!' Eric cried. 'She's been drugged! They've knocked her out cold!' He looked in the fridge, and found a small brown medical-looking bottle. 'Look at this! Cow tranquillisers! That stuck-up little madam, Evelina Semolina! She's knocked our Eunice out of the game!'

Mam was shaking Eunice harder and harder, so that Eunice's arms were waving and her head flopping about all over the place. 'Don't let us down now! We have to win! You have to WAKE UP, EUNICE!!!' Mam was growing desparate.

'ZZZZzzzzzz, zzzzzz, zzzzzZZZZZZZZZZZZZ,' Eunice went.

'It's hopeless, Marjorie,' Eric said, taking hold of Mam. She was starting to slap Eunice's face. Eric picked up the nearest vase. He yanked out all of the gorgeous roses and chucked the cold water in Eunice's face. Some of it got me. Still Eunice didn't stir a muscle.

'ZZZZZzzzzzZZZZZ!'

'She's dead!' shrieked Mam. 'Oh, don't tell me she's dead! We'll never win anything then!'

'She's not dead,' Eric sighed. 'She's just up to her eyeballs in cow tranquillisers. There's no way she's going out on that stage tonight.'

We three looked at each other. Our hearts were sinking. We had ground to a standstill with shock and disappointment.

After all this! After everything! We had come so

far – and only for this! To be hobbled by poisoned strawberry-flavoured semolina fizz!

'That's it, then,' Eric said. 'I'll have to tell them: we have to pull out of the contest.'

'Get a doctor in!' Mam said. 'Get some help! Wake her up!'

Eric started to go. He paused in the doorway. He looked at me and then he looked at Mam. He looked at me again. 'There is, of course, something we *could* do, you know . . .'

We stared back at him. 'What?'

'Even with Eunice asleep like this. There is a way that we could still win the *Diva Wars*. We could show them that we're not defeated yet.'

'WHAT?' Mam shouted, impatiently. 'What can we do?'

Eric smiled and said, very slowly: 'Helen could go on by herself.'

Chapter Twenty-Four

So this is me, now.

I've brought you right up to date in the story of our success.

Here I am, backstage. I'm waiting to step through those doors and walk out onto the stage.

All alone.

I'm dressed up in the outfit we chose. Me and Eunice were going to wear exactly the same, as we always did. It's a sharp little frock in black and red and, I must say, I look fantastic in it. Mam wept when I was all ready to go out and leave the dressing room.

'You look beautiful,' she told me. 'My Helen. You're really beautiful.'

Eunice was still sprawled out on the sofa. 'ZZZzzzzzzzzZZZZZZZZ,' she went, by way of encouragement.

Eric hugged me, looking all teary. 'Knock 'em dead, midget,' he said.

I was barefoot. I didn't have any of my own shoes to go out on stage with! The only shoes we had were our special ones; our Mary-Sue shoes. What a relief it had been, to undo the buckles and straps, and set myself free from Eunice and our subterfuge.

'You have to be very brave,' Eric told me, as I prepared to meet my public. 'Not only for singing your song and wowing them. But for facing them and telling them that it was all a big mistake. That you aren't Siamese any longer. You'll have to be brave and tell them that you're a solo diva now.'

I nodded, trying to be brave enough.

'ZZZZzzz,' said Eunice.

'My little Helen,' Mam said. 'Fancy! Going out there alone!'

Agatha Staynes walked into our dressing room just then. She took one look at me and screamed. 'What's happened? Has there been an accident?' She was completely horrified to see Eunice and me separated.

It took some time to calm her down. Mam forced some champagne down her throat.

As Agatha thrashed around deliriously, and eventually returned to consciousness, our TV monitor crackled into life.

'We're on air!' Eric cried excitedly. 'Look! It's all starting!'

We turned, transfixed by the tacky title sequence. And then . . .

'Crikey! Look at my mother!' Eric cried out, and started to laugh. Tonight's *Diva Wars* opened in great style, with Marlene giving it her tiny all.

'Come on, Agatha!' Mam shouted into the old woman's shocked face. 'You have to be out there! You have to pull yourself together!'

'But . . . but . . . they're separated!' she gibbered. 'What's happened?'

There were a lot of explanations that needed to be given. But there wasn't much time. We all looked at Eric, and I'll love him for ever for his quick-thinking. 'It's a *miracle*!' he yelled. 'Praise be!'

'ZZZZZzzzzzzz, zzzzzzz, zzzzz,' went Eunice.

And so we were bundled out of the dressing room, leaving Eunice behind. Into the studios, into the heart of the music and lights and excitement. I was kissed goodbye by Agatha, Mam and Eric. And before I knew it, I was led backstage, while they took their seats out front.

Now I'm ready to face the music.

Alone.

Maybe they will all scream.

Siamese double-act splits, live on TV! I can already see the headlines.

Maybe Trevor Rotter will go bananas and try to have me disqualified again. Maybe Evelina Semolina will go crazy with frustration, that we've still managed to get into the show!

I feel very tiny, back here in the darkness.

I'm waiting for the music to start.

Perhaps I shouldn't be here. Perhaps I don't deserve this.

Perhaps I don't want this after all.

This: walking out onto the huge glassy stage . . . It's as sheer and as wide as an ice rink.

I can't see the audience. They are beyond the ring of brilliant lights. But I know the crowd is immense. I stare back at them, bravely, undeterred. I know they are muttering to each other as they realise the truth. I am a girl alone. There's only me here. They are shocked to see me like this, standing alone. And I know my mam and Eric are sitting there, holding their breath. And Marlene is there, her heart still thumping hard from singing her own song. And, beyond all of them, I know that millions of people are watching me at home. Millions of them! Watching me, on my own! About to sing my song at last!

They're egging me on to be a star.

But I want to be a travel agent. With a smart

blouse and a computer, and brochures. Talking about beaches and planes and places to stay. Isn't that what I really want?

Not *Diva Wars*. Not all this showbiz stuff . . .

But now the music is starting. The bassline is thumping through the stage and right through my body. Here comes the melody. Here comes my cue . . . I have a real gift for singing. I know that, and I know I have to do this. Right now.

No tricks this time. No lies or gimmicks.

Just me and my voice. In the limelight.

Standing on my own two feet.

Wish me luck!

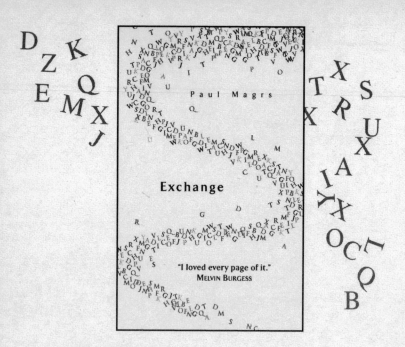

Paul Magrs

Exchange

"I loved every page of it."
MELVIN BURGESS

Following the death of his parents,
16-year-old Simon moves into his grandparents'
claustrophobic bungalow, which quickly
becomes a refuge from his bullying peers. United
by their voracious appetite for books, Simon and
his grandmother stumble across the Great Big
Book Exchange – a bookshop with a difference.
There they meet impulsive, gothic Kelly and her
boss, Terrance – and the friendships forged in
the Great Big Book Exchange result in startling
and unsettling consequences for them all.

978-1-41691-663-5